Look what people are saying about Leslie Kelly

"Kelly is a top writer, and this is another excellent book. 4 ½ stars."
—*RT Book Reviews* on *Play with Me*

"A hip contemporary romance packed with great one-liners! 4 ½ stars."
—*RT Book Reviews* on *Terms of Surrender*

"*One Wild Wedding Night* features sexy and fun stories with likable characters, only to end with a sexy story that floors me with how well it resonates with me. Oh, this one is definitely wild, but even better, it also aims for the heart."
—*Mrs. Giggles*

"Whoa baby, *Overexposed* is hot stuff! Ms. Kelly employs a great deal of heart and humor to achieve balance with the incendiary romance. Great characters, many of whom fans will recognize, and a vibrant narrative kept this reader glued to each and every word. *Overexposed* is without a doubt one of the better Blaze books I have read to date."
—*The Romance Reader's Connection*

"Filled with humor and heart, *Slow Hands,* by Leslie Kelly, is a complete delight... The cross-purpose conversations and situations that result are laugh-out-loud funny. The romantic entanglements are highly emotional, and the large cast is expertly handled. 4 ½ stars!"
—*RT Book Reviews*

Dear Reader,

Believe it or not, although I'm a big fan of many of Shakespeare's plays, I had never, until very recently, read *A Midsummer Night's Dream.* Nor had I ever seen one of the movie adaptations. But when I started talking about ideas for a Blazing-hot summer read with my fabulous editor, that story just leaped into my mind. Once I'd read it, I knew I had to tackle the basic premise in Blaze. Add in a few twisted, sexy fortunes in a fortune cookie, and I had a perfect setup for lots of spicy dreams.

I love writing my books with little "Easter Eggs" for readers to find and grin over. So there are some *Midsummer* references in this book, beyond the overall storyline and characters. I hope you have fun finding them—and that you enjoy reading about Mimi and Xander's sexy midsummer-night adventures!

Happy reading!

Leslie Kelly

Leslie Kelly

BLAZING MIDSUMMER NIGHTS

TORONTO NEW YORK LONDON
AMSTERDAM PARIS SYDNEY HAMBURG
STOCKHOLM ATHENS TOKYO MILAN MADRID
PRAGUE WARSAW BUDAPEST AUCKLAND

Recycling programs for this product may not exist in your area.

ISBN-13: 978-0-373-79693-9

BLAZING MIDSUMMER NIGHTS

This edition published by arrangement with Harlequin Books S.A.

For questions and comments about the quality of this book please contact us at Customer_eCare@Harlequin.ca.

www.Harlequin.com

Printed in U.S.A.

ABOUT THE AUTHOR

Leslie Kelly has written dozens of books and novellas for Harlequin Blaze, Temptation and HQN. Known for her sparkling dialogue, fun characters and depth of emotion, her books have been honored with numerous awards, including a National Readers' Choice Award, an *RT Book Reviews* Award and three nominations for the highest award in romance, the RWA RITA® Award. Leslie lives in Maryland with her own romantic hero, Bruce, and their three daughters. Visit her online at www.lesliekelly.com.

Books by Leslie Kelly

HARLEQUIN BLAZE

347—OVEREXPOSED
369—ONE WILD WEDDING NIGHT
402—SLOW HANDS
408—HEATED RUSH
447—BLAZING BEDTIME STORIES
"My, What a Big...You Have!"
501—MORE BLAZING BEDTIME STORIES
"Once Upon a Mattress"
521—PLAY WITH ME
537—BLAZING BEDTIME STORIES, VOLUME V
"A Prince of a Guy"
567—ANOTHER WILD WEDDING NIGHT
616—TERMS OF SURRENDER
650—IT HAPPENED ONE CHRISTMAS
663—ONCE UPON A VALENTINE
"Sleeping with a Beauty"

To Brit Lit teachers everywhere…
you make Shakespeare fun!

1

SOMEONE ONCE SAID that the course of true love never did run smooth. As Mimi Burdette watched two of her good friends sway together in a romantic dance, however, she had to disagree. Because the true love between this couple had been obvious to everyone who knew them, almost from the moment they'd met.

"They look like a prince and princess," murmured Anna, her neighbor, friend, landlady and tonight's hostess.

"Considering the setting, maybe a fairy king and queen."

She wasn't kidding. The woods surrounding the backyard of the old plantation house just outside of Athens had been turned into a mythical forest. As dusk fell and a thousand twinkle lights began to gleam in the night, everyone at the engagement party slowed to appreciate the beauty all around them.

A trio of musicians softly strummed their instruments, the lyrical notes riding a warm, summer breeze. The Spanish moss hanging from the live oaks gleamed silver under the evening dew and the firefly-soft lighting.

Magnolias the size of dinner plates dotted the trees, looking like a thousand full moons, filling the air with their evocative scent. Lanterns hung from the lowest branches of the graceful pines, and the arches of a dozen arbors were draped with writhing, sweet-smelling jasmine and heavily laden grapevines.

Okay, the vines and fruit were fake. But what an effect!

"You *really* outdid yourself," Mimi said to Anna, who stood watching the proceedings, wearing a smile.

The older woman, dressed as always in colorful, flowing robes, merely shrugged. "Setting the stage for romance is easy when the people involved are meant for each other like Duke and Lyssa." She chuckled. "Of course, it didn't hurt that I'm helping with the costumes and props for the downtown theater group's production of *A Midsummer Night's Dream.*"

With her filmy, billowing clothes, and her long ash-gray hair, loose and wavy and entwined with flowers, Anna looked more like a hippie than a retiree. So maybe it wasn't so surprising that she could take a normal backyard, ringed by normal Georgia woods, and turn it into something out of a storybook.

"Anyway, it was just a few lights, some fabric—easy."

"Maybe for you, but other than advertising, the creative wiring was left out of my genetic code. To me, this looks like pure sorcery and magic."

The soon-to-be bride and groom deserved a magical wedding. They were wonderful people, and she already missed having them as neighbors. They'd already moved into their new house, but until a week ago, had lived right across the hall from her own first-floor apartment in this grand old estate home.

Anna and her husband, Ralph—dubbed Obi-Wan because of his love for all things *Star Wars* and his sage, all-knowing demeanor—had bought the place decades ago and raised their family here. Once the kids were gone, they'd divided the three-story mansion into six small apartments, figuring the rental income would keep them nicely provided for in their retirement.

With the unit across from Mimi's vacant, and another unrented one on the second floor, the big house was feeling empty. Plus, Anna and Obi-Wan's volatile marriage was on the rocks again. Obi-Wan's one fault was his jealous streak. He was always accusing other men of being after his wife. His latest accusation had angered Anna enough that she had moved into one of the vacant units to teach him a lesson.

In this economy, three rentals not bringing in any money was not a good thing. She had to wonder where Anna had come up with the funds to throw this engagement party for her former tenants. Mimi had offered to help pay—she could certainly afford it and would have loved to help—but Anna's pride wouldn't allow her to accept. The most she would allow was the use of Mimi's nice discount on much of the food.

Sometimes it really paid to be the daughter of the owner of a chain of grocery stores. Not to mention being the head of marketing for said grocery store chain, with an express ticket to the executive offices of her family's business.

Some people wondered why she lived here, in a small apartment in an old house, when she could afford to buy her own home, or sponge off her parents at their estate. But Mimi loved this place, loved the history of it. More importantly, she loved the sense of community she found here, where she was free to be herself and didn't have to wear the socialite hat, or the business executive one. She could just be Mimi.

"Oh," Anna said, snapping her fingers as she remembered something. "You're going to have new neighbors. My daughter, Helen, and her little boy are moving from Atlanta next weekend, taking the vacant unit on two. And I rented the apartment across from yours today."

"Really? That's wonderful," Mimi said, surprised.

"I invited the new tenant to come tonight, but he didn't want to intrude—he moved in this afternoon."

"You must be so glad," she said, relieved to know one financial burden had been lifted from her landlords' shoulders. She doubted they'd take rent money from their daughter, who had gone through a bad divorce last year.

"One B is a real hottie," Anna said, her eyebrows waggling.

"There are more important things than hotness."

Definitely more important. She'd been involved with superhot guys in the past and had the psychological burn scars to prove it. The last supersexy, relied-only-on-his-looks guy she'd dated had ended up "borrowing" her credit card and buying a matching pair of his-and-her motorcycles.

That had been bad. Worse? Mimi hadn't been the *her.*

No way was she stepping close to the flames again. Now when she looked at a man, she was more interested in steadiness, self-confidence and brains. If those things came in nice-looking packages, okay, but looks alone just didn't cut it.

Fortunately, it was possible to have all of the above. She only had to look across the crowded party at her own golden-haired escort to see that.

Dimitri was perfect. He was everything she'd been telling herself she needed, and was nothing like the men who'd hurt her in the past. He'd also been hand-picked for her by her own father, who was notoriously hard to please. Normally, that would be a bad thing; she didn't like doing what was expected of her, and knew her father to be a bully. But considering her bad luck with romance, and her efforts to improve her relationship with her dad—who stood firmly in the path of her going where she wanted to go professionally, i.e., right into his office once he retired—it seemed like a smart move.

The icing on the cake? Dimitri was also very handsome.

But handsome doesn't always equal hot. And enjoying being with someone definitely doesn't always lead to physical heat.

She sighed deeply, wishing that little voice in her head would shut up, even while acknowledging the words were true.

But it didn't matter—handsome was enough. Handsome was movie-star good looks, good manners, holding the door. Handsome was every hair in place, jaw smoothly shaven and a nice suit. Handsome was self-confidence borne of being admired by everyone who knew him, and inspiring fantasies of Prince Charming in just about every woman who saw him. Handsome was a good-night kiss with enough tongue to be provocative but not enough to be impolite.

Handsome was Dimitri.

Hot was…something else.

Hot was sexy, rugged and edgy. Hot was unpredictable. Hot smelled sweaty and male, not doused with expensive cologne. Hot had thick muscles that gave proof of utter strength and could make any woman feel feminine by contrast. Hot had an edge of danger, wasn't always courteous, didn't treat a lover like a fragile object. Hot had a deep voice, knowing eyes and a stubbled jaw that every woman wanted roughing up her inner thighs. Hot would ensnare a woman…mind, body and soul.

She fanned herself, acknowledging the truth. Handsome she had. Hot she hadn't seen in a very long time.

More importantly: handsome she *should* have. Hot she should stay away from.

She shook off the mental images. Enough with the hot fantasies. Handsome reality was bringing her a glass of wine, drawing the appreciative stares of every person with a uterus.

He was hers if she wanted him. *And you want him. Damn it, you'd be crazy not to want him!*

But she was beginning to wonder. Heck, she hadn't even been the one to invite him here tonight. Anna had bumped into him at the store and extended the invitation. Mimi had no idea why he'd accepted, considering he didn't know anybody here except her. Since he'd said yes, he'd naturally expected Mimi to be his date, which *should* make any woman extremely happy.

"Okay, Miss Smarty-Pants, if you're not about looks, care to explain your date over there?"

"You invited him," she pointed out.

"Only because you've gone out with him a few times."

"I know, my family swears he's perfect for me. And he is very good-looking," she admitted. Then, speaking more to herself, she voiced the concern that had been niggling at her. "But there's also something called chemistry."

"Hate to break it to ya, but you two ain't got it."

She sighed. "Is it that obvious?"

"Only to an expert like me."

And to Mimi. She'd already figured out that good looks didn't always inspire sparks, and dating someone wasn't the same as wanting to go to bed with him. If it were, she and Dimitri would probably be sleeping together, or perhaps even engaged, which was what her father was pushing for. Pushing hard.

Dimitri was a new executive with Burdette Quality Foods, the family business. He was also her Dad's right-hand man. Cultured, handsome, well-educated. The perfect guy in every way.

But perfect for her?

Anna shook her head and tsked. "Honey, it's obvious you're experiencing a small sexual dry spell."

"Small? Try Sahara-sized," she admitted, wondering, not for the first time, if there was something wrong with her.

"So, sex camel, what are you looking for, a Brad Pitt or Johnny Depp oasis?"

Dimitri would probably be considered every bit as handsome as those men. Still, there was no fire. When he kissed her, she always thought, *well, that's nice.*

But she never had the urge to rip off his pressed shirt, shove him against a wall and thrust her tongue down his throat. And they'd never done anything more than kiss. He hadn't pushed, and she hadn't wanted him to. Because, for a sex camel, nice sex wasn't an oasis, it was just the last few drops of water from a nearly empty canteen.

If she really wanted an oasis, she needed *hot.*

Forget it. Heat burns. A lukewarm canteen is good enough.

"I honestly don't know," she finally admitted. "He's everything I should want."

"But not what you need? Not what you crave?"

Needing and craving didn't begin to describe what she felt for Dimitri. Respecting and appreciating did. "Like I said, there's more to life."

"You tell yourself that the next time a gorgeous, hot, half-naked man lands at your feet."

"I think I'll go for a walk during the next thunderstorm. I'd have a better chance of getting struck by lightning."

"Thunderstorm?" Dimitri asked. "It doesn't look like rain."

Glad he hadn't overheard their entire conversation, Mimi took the glass of wine he offered, murmuring, "Thank you."

"You're welcome. How about a dance when you're finished?"

Dancing under the stars with a handsome man. It should sound heavenly. But instead it sounded…just okay. As okay as everything else in her life lately.

Okay is fine. Okay is better than wounded and

lonely. Okay is better than wondering what the hell is wrong with you since the last few rounds of ring-around-the-relationship ended with you in the used-and-heartbroken seat.

She'd been following her libido instead of her brain and had lived to regret it. So her brain needed to be in charge from now on. And her brain said okay was good enough.

"Sure, thanks," she said, lowering the glass.

She let Dimitri lead her to the flagstone patio, which was being used for dancing. Mimi held her breath, looking up at his handsome face—all slashing, *GQ*-magazine-cover cheekbones, haughty brows, dark green eyes that watched her closely. She was waiting for a frisson of sensation, a spark at the brush of his tall, lean body against her own, but it just didn't happen.

Maybe it never will. Maybe acknowledging that he's handsome and smart, and liking him will do.

She did like him, and respected him. She doubted he'd hurt her—the fact that she wasn't desperate for him should be enough to insulate her from too much pain if things went south. And it would certainly make things nice in terms of the business, not to mention her rocky relationship with her dad.

In this day and age, no self-respecting woman would marry a man just to please her father, and Mimi wouldn't, either. But considering her old man swore she'd said every word in the dictionary except "Dada" as an infant, just to spite him, she didn't think extending an olive branch was such a bad thing. It wasn't just wanting to keep things smooth at work. She also didn't want to fight with him because she knew it upset her mother, who'd been playing the role of peacekeeper since Mimi took her first steps. So would it really be such a hardship to let herself drift into a relationship with a man most women would consider a Greek god, who was also rich, smart and nice?

No. It wouldn't.

It was time to rid herself of the I-want-it-hot fantasies and move into the next phase of her life. The settle-down-and-marry-a-nice-handsome-man-and-have-a-family phase. Which meant maybe it was time to move her relationship with Dimitri up a notch…and closer to her bedroom.

She thought about it. The party would wind down in an hour or two. Afterward, she could invite him into her apartment for a drink. They'd kiss. She'd move close, let her breasts brush against his chest. Tangle her legs between his. She wouldn't resist when he slid his hand up her thigh, edging her dress ever higher. Until he reached her… "Oh, hell," she mumbled.

"What's wrong?" he asked.

"Nothing," she insisted, feeling heat stain her cheeks.

Nothing except she was in no way dressed for seduction. Oh, sure, she was on the outside. But underneath her slinky, sexy dress, she wore what every other self-respecting American woman who didn't want a single bulge showing wore: Spanx.

She'd loved this dress the minute she saw it, though it had been a size smaller than she usually wore. A pair of superstrong control-top panties had seemed a small price to pay…but they weren't going to lend themselves to a romantic atmosphere. He'd probably have to get power tools to drag them off her.

Only one thing to do. Ditch the drawers.

The evening was getting late, it was dark, people were drinking. Who'd notice if she switched into something sexy and her dress suddenly fit a little too tightly? Nobody, that's who. And maybe doing it—getting ready for seduction, feeling the silky glide of lingerie against her most intimate parts—would get her in the mood to act on her plan to seduce him.

"Would you excuse me? I need to run inside for a minute."

To pry off my underwear.

"Of course," he said, releasing her. No argument, no suggestion that he go, too, so they could continue their dance in private. How—*boring*—refreshing.

Thrusting aside those thoughts, she turned away from him toward the house. But she hadn't taken one step when she heard a woman nearby whisper in a loud, tipsy voice, "Whoa, mama, who's that?"

Curious about the comment, which sounded as though it should have been accompanied by a purr, she glanced toward the gate, and her breath caught in her throat.

Anna stood there, and beside her was a stranger. A tall, dark-haired stranger, wearing low-slung jeans and *nothing* else.

The jeans looked good. The *nothing,* fantastic.

He was shirtless, shoeless, sweaty. His slick, tanned body gleamed under the twinkle lights, lines of oh-so-interesting skin striped with equally interesting shadow. His broad shoulders looked Atlas-size, and his thickly muscled arms flexed as he swiped a hand through his jet-black hair.

She couldn't make out whether he was as handsome of face as he was of body. But she definitely noted that his six-pack abs were so perfect they ought to be sold in a liquor store and come with a warning label.

Whoa, mama, indeed.

"Mimi? Are you all right?"

She tore her attention off the stranger and glanced at Dimitri, who was watching her curiously.

"I'm fine," she told Mr. Handsome.

But, heaven help her, she could not stop wondering about the identity of the new arrival.

Aka: Mr. Hot.

TALK ABOUT MAKING a bad first impression on his new neighbors. Not only was Xander McKinley *so* not the garden party type, but he was also bare-chested, sweaty and probably stunk from having lugged boxes all evening.

He had fully intended to stay inside tonight, to ignore the party going on in his new backyard. He was a stranger to these people, and while it had been nice of his landlady to extend the invitation, he hadn't even considered intruding. He still hadn't gotten his head wrapped around the whole Southern-gentility thing, since Georgia was like a different world from Chicago. But he knew it wasn't mannerly to barge in on a party when the invite had only been extended out of politeness. So he'd planned to just finish hauling in the last of his stuff, which he'd picked up from the storage unit this afternoon, then unpack a few boxes and settle into his new home.

Unfortunately, settling in hadn't included hooking

his new key to his key ring. So when he'd run outside to grab one last thing out of the truck—sans shirt and shoes—he'd also found himself sans key. And locked out.

"I'm so sorry about this," he repeated to his new landlady.

Anna waved away his apology. "I should think you'd know how to get in without a key, being a dashing firefighter and all."

"I didn't think you'd want me ramming the door down."

"Best not. Anyway, it's just as well, since it forced you to come out and meet everyone," she said.

He gestured toward his sweaty, bare chest. "I'm not exactly dressed for a party."

"Well, I won't let you back into your place until you promise to come back after you've gotten cleaned up."

"I don't know…."

"I do. No more arguments." The woman led him to a row of chairs in a gazebo, grabbing an oversized purse that was covered with peace signs and jingled with every movement. "I don't have a key to your front door with me, but I have a master that fits all the secret doors."

"*Secret* doors?"

"You probably didn't notice it—every unit has one. The one in your unit is inside what's now your bedroom closet. It leads into the screened porch." She grabbed a jangling ring of keys and removed a small, antique-looking one. "Here it is. Go through the porch and head for the door in the far right corner."

She gestured toward the porch, and he glanced over.

There were about fifty people at the party, many of them milling around outside the back door, and he was going to have to go through all of them. Great. Wonderful. *Note to self—don't go out shirtless and shoeless unless you know you can get back in.*

He reached for the key, but before he could take it, something caught his attention. Or, rather, someone.

He whistled. "Who is *she?*" he mumbled, not even realizing he'd said it out loud.

There were a lot of women here. Attractive women. The South definitely had its share of them. But this one actually made him forget where he was and what he was saying. He could only stand there, staring, as she walked toward the screened-in porch.

With her back to the decorated lawn and woods, she was almost haloed by the thousands of tiny lights. She looked like some kind of magical creature stepping out of a storybook, and he had to blink a few times to rid his mind of the imagery.

He could shake off the magic, but no amount of blinking could change the fact that she was stunning. Or that she looked like she belonged to the night—to nature and the woods and everything mystical.

The woman was tall. Her silky dress was long and shimmery, the color of soft, springy moss, and it clung to a curvy body that would make a man drop to his knees and howl. Her thick hair fell down her back in a tumble of waves and was a mixture of earthy colors—mostly red, but with some gold and brown strewn in there as well. He couldn't make out her features in this lighting and from this distance, but he saw a mouth curved up into a smile.

He'd thought earlier how hot it was for a summer night. But he hadn't even understood the meaning of the word until he'd spied her across the party. Because a blast of heat had hit him square in the chest just watching her cross the lawn.

"That's Mimi Burdette." His landlady smiled, her gaze shifting back and forth between him and the redhead, who'd disappeared into the screened porch. "Would you like me to introduce you when you come back?"

Oh, hell to the yeah. But something made him ask, "Is she here alone?"

"She's single," the woman replied without hesitation. "Totally available."

Hard to believe, but everybody had a down spell now and then. "Interesting," he said, more to himself than to Anna.

He hadn't even been thinking about meeting a woman; the idea of romance was so far down on his list it wasn't on the first page. New job, new home, new state, fresh start—yeah, that was his focus. Having nothing left in Chicago, he'd moved south, determined to make sure he did what he'd promised his parents he'd do before they'd both died last year—go out and start over somewhere new. Find a life for himself. One that didn't include sadness and loss and family responsibilities that had kept him close to home for nearly all of his thirty years.

Hell, maybe a woman could be part of that new life. Just because he hadn't been looking didn't mean he should walk the other way if an interesting one crossed his path. And an interesting one had most definitely just crossed his path.

"Mimi, huh?" The name was too cute for such a sensual-looking woman and he had to wonder if it was a nickname.

"She's fabulous," Anna gushed. "Daughter to a grocery store magnate. Very wealthy and successful."

Oh, great. Just the type of woman he did *not* need. He stiffened, unable to help it.

It wasn't that he didn't like rich people. He made it a point to never judge anyone based on their checkbook balance, be it written in red ink or in black. It was just that, working as a Chicago firefighter, he had met more than a few wealthy women who wanted to walk on the wild side with somebody who had a dangerous job. He'd once participated in a bachelor auction to benefit a kids' charity. The Junior League set had treated all the men like meat in a butcher shop. The sixtyish cougar who'd bought a date with him hadn't quite reached the level of sexual assault, but she'd come close, and he'd sworn he'd never date a woman with money. Rich, spoiled and young probably wasn't too much different from rich, spoiled and old. *So forget her.*

"Thanks, but I don't think so," he said, disappointment flooding him. Anna's brow shot up, and confusion creased her brow. Not wanting to explain, Xander added, "And thanks for the key. I'll return it soon."

"Okay, see you in a little while." Then, clearing her throat, Anna added, "Remember, through the screen porch, to the small, old-fashioned door in the far *left* corner."

Left? Yeesh. Good thing she'd repeated herself—

he'd been thinking right. Or, more accurately, he *hadn't* been thinking right...not since he'd spied that stunning figure in green.

Xander nodded, then headed for the porch. There were at least a dozen people inside. He didn't see a reddish head, but he probably would once he stepped into the shadowy alcove. Despite having decided that some rich Southern belle whose looks clawed at his guts wasn't on his shortlist of people to meet, he couldn't deny he wanted to see her close up. Mainly he wanted to see her eyes. Were they green, the same mossy shade as her dress? Or a rich amber-brown?

Or maybe they're pinched, cold, bloodshot.

That would probably be a good thing. Because then he would see she wasn't as attractive as he imagined, but just a normal, rich, bored, jaded young woman. Not some magical fantasy creature spun out of summer moonlight.

As it turned out, though, he didn't get the chance to see her up close. Because, as he made his way across the screened porch, he realized she wasn't inside. She must have slipped back out when he wasn't looking.

Smiling and nodding at the several people who said hello, he headed for the back left corner. The door was tiny, as Anna had warned, and was nearly hidden by a large, potted plant. Sliding the key into the old-fashioned lock, he entered, seeing a small, dark passage before him.

Inside, clothes hung in front of his face—more felt than seen, since it was so dark. He must have hung up more things than he'd remembered, because the closet was more full than he'd expected. Of course, it could just seem that way because he was coming in from this side angle.

He pushed past his things, noting the soft, delicate scent in the air. Whoever had rented this place before him must have left behind some sachet or air freshener—his clothes sure didn't smell like the flowery stuff that filled his every breath.

Reaching the doors that led to his new bedroom, he saw one was slightly ajar, and that the room beyond was well-lit. Strange. He didn't remember putting a bulb in the new lamp he'd picked up for his bedside table.

He had just put up his hand to push the door the rest of the way open, when he heard a voice.

"Soft and pretty, sultry and sexy or hot and raunchy?"

He froze. That voice had come from his bedroom, and he knew damn well he hadn't even hooked up a TV or radio, much less left it turned on.

"What's it going to take to turn you on?"

Sexy voices of strange women standing in my bedroom would be his first answer. Though, why said strange woman would be in his bedroom, he had no idea. Had a pair of guests crept inside, thinking to slip into what had been an empty unit until earlier today, to grab a midparty quickie?

"Do you like what you see?" she purred.

He waited for a male voice to answer, but heard nothing. Miss Purrs-A-Lot was either talking to herself, or the guy she was with had been struck mute while he tried to decide between pretty, sexy or raunchy.

Frankly, so had Xander. All he could wonder was if there was an option D, for "all of the above."

Well, he'd also been struck mute by the realization that he was playing the role of voyeur in this sexy drama.

"I somehow suspect you'll like pretty and soft, not sexy," she said, her voice a little less throaty, a little less wicked. In fact, she sounded almost...disappointed. Which lent credence to his theory that she was entirely alone.

He rubbed his forehead, racking his brain to figure this out. A voice was coming from his bedroom. A female voice. A throaty, attractive female voice. A throaty, attractive female voice talking about something very sexy. To herself.

Wondering if he'd taken a wrong turn and ended up in a male fantasyland, or was being set up for some kind of X-rated *Punk'd* episode, he pushed the door open another inch and looked into the room. He couldn't see far, because his line of sight was blocked by the woman staring at her reflection in the mirror on the other—closed—closet door. Yep. She had definitely been *talking* to herself; to her reflection, anyway.

Then he realized...it was her. The redhead whose eyes, he now saw, were so blue they looked [illegible]let. The one in the green dress. Only, now, she w[illegible]t wearing that green dress. She was—*holy shit*[illegible]ly naked.

The long strands of her red hair [illegible]allen forward over her soft, bare shoulders, co[illegible] much of a lacy black bra. And covering the [illegible]that bra was covering.

Too bad.

No, it's not, jackass[illegible]se he didn't know if his [illegible]g what he suspected was heart could have tak[illegible] an utterly perfect pair of breasts. Just spying the rest of her body was enough to rob him of breath. And coherent thought.

The hair played peek-a-boo with the bra. But below that was nothing but smooth, soft-looking, pale, feminine skin. Miles and miles of it.

Her bare midriff drew his eyes downward, to the indentation of her small waist, then the flare of her hips. Those hips were covered by two thin straps of silky fabric—dark green, lacy—that descended into a V of shimmery material that covered her groin. Long, supple legs went on forever, or to the floor, ending in a pair of sexy, spike-heeled black shoes.

"So I guess a thong might be overdoing it," she said.

A thong could never overdo it in his book.

"Too bad. This thing doesn't look too shabby," she said with a sigh. She turned, glancing at her reflection, checking out the rear view.

Oh, man, what a view. The strip-of-fabric-pretending-to-be-underwear slid between two delectable cheeks, and Xander nearly choked, sure he'd never seen a more perfect ass.

Sud[illegible]nly realizing what he was doing—playing Peepin[illegible]om—he slammed his eyes shut. Sure, the woman [illegible]ecided to come into his bedroom to do her lingeri[illegible]ssment, for some weird reason, but that didn't mean[illegible]ould stand here in the dark like some perv, squirmi[illegible]atch a peek.

He tried to fi[illegible]ut what to do. How did one handle this type of s[illegible]? Should he go back the way he'd come, hoping [illegible]ldn't hear him, then go tell his landlady that som[illegible] with a great ass and a Godiva complex was trespassing in his place? Or maybe he ought to get out there and confront her before her boyfriend showed up to decide whether he liked her thong? He hadn't even slept in his brand-new bed himself yet; he sure didn't want another couple christening it.

Especially not if the other couple was *that* woman and any other man on the planet than himself.

He could have answered one question for her—*yes, oh, hell, yes on her current underwear.* If the guy was straight and breathing, he'd like the damn thong. In fact, as for himself, well, he couldn't think about much except how much he wanted to tug that shiny green fabric out from between those luscious curves. With his teeth.

You gotta get out of here.

Yeah. Pronto.

Even though the lighting was low in the closet, and he couldn't see well, he knew he'd have to at least open his eyes to make sure he didn't poke himself in the face with a hanger. So he risked a peek, opening just the left one. He hadn't turned away from the crack in the door, so he got a full-on image of what she was up to.

She was up to dropping her panties.

"Whoa, stop right there!" he barked, not even having made the decision to reveal himself. Instinct just propelled him out into the bedroom.

She let out a little scream, and he opened his mouth to tell her he wasn't some kind of attacker. But before he could speak, and before she could dive for her clothes or dart for the door, his foot caught the edge of the dresser, and he fell flat on the floor, landing right at her sexy feet.

And looking up at a most *interesting* view.

2

LOOKING DOWN AT the incredibly gorgeous, hot, sexy, shirtless man lying at her feet, Mimi at first thought she'd had one too many glasses of wine and was seeing things. But considering she'd only had one, she doubted she was intoxicated.

Her second thought was that she was about to be attacked.

She grabbed a vase off her dresser. It was a heavy, leaded crystal thing, that would probably crack the pervert's skull open. She came close—so incredibly close—to dropping it on his head, when a voice whispered in her mind, *He's Mr. Hot. He was at the party. Anna knows him.*

It seemed crazy to suppose that before attacking, a sexual predator ditched his clothes and socialized at parties in his victims' backyards. So who was he?

"Who are you and what were you doing in my closet?" she asked, still not letting go of the vase.

"*Your* closet...?" he mumbled, rising to his hands and knees. On all fours, he turned his head from side to side, looking around the room, and added, "I'm in the wrong apartment."

"No shit, Sherlock. Now who are you?"

He lifted his head to look up at her. And his big brown eyes—gorgeous, beautiful, velvety-brown eyes that were ringed by the longest lashes she'd ever seen on a man—got even wider.

That was when she remembered she was naked but for her bra. And that he was kneeling at her feet. About eye level with…

"Oh, my God," she groaned, lunging for her dresser. She plopped the vase on it, grabbed her robe and thrust her arms inside, quickly wrapping it around her body.

She couldn't stop shaking. Adrenaline had put her on high alert. Now humiliation and embarrassment were doing their darnedest to make her quiver into a ball of mush.

Had she really just flashed her goodies to a complete stranger? And, for the briefest, most wicked second, had she not been tantalized by the image of that incredibly hot, sexy stranger moving a few inches closer for a more intimate look?

She'd been in here planning to seduce a nice man she'd been dating and was about as aroused as a stick of wood. But playing a Sharon Stone-type game of peek-a-crotch with a gorgeous mystery man got her all warm and melty down there?

She clenched her thighs together. Yeah. Warm and melty. Like chocolate left in the sun.

Just waiting to be tasted.

She winced and clenched harder. What on earth was

wrong with her? "This can't be happening," she said with a moan.

"Tell me about it."

The stranger, all slick-skinned, broad-chested and rippling muscles, slowly rose to his feet. He continued to look around the room, shaking his head slowly, as if in a daze.

Up close, he was more attractive—not to mention at least twenty degrees hotter—than he had been from across the party. His jaw was so square, his face so lean and masculine. Such masculinity shouldn't have looked right with the accompanying long lashes and the downright full lips, but managed to come across as perfect.

"This really *isn't* my bedroom." He still sounded thoroughly confused.

"I think we've established that. It's my bedroom. Did you not happen to notice the pink sheets and lingerie?"

Of course he noticed the lingerie, idiot.

Feeling her face flame, and the rest of her get a little warmer, too, she tightened her arms around her waist, conscious of how silky and thin the robe was. Could he see the pucker of her nipples against the cloth? Was there any way he could tell that her thighs were quivering and she badly wanted to lean against the edge of the bed for support?

"I noticed," he admitted, his eyes darkening.

She licked her lips, reminded herself to breathe. "How did you get in here?" It made no sense. Hadn't he been outside at the party when she'd entered the screen porch? And while she'd left the door unlocked on the way out earlier, she'd flipped the lock when coming back in.

He lifted his hand, showing her a small key.

She gaped. "Where did you get that?"

"From Anna. I locked myself out of my apartment."

All the breath left her lungs as she suddenly realized who he was. Not some random, lost party guest. Not a drunk who might forget this night ever happened. Not a handsome stranger she would never have to see again. No. She'd just come face-to-coochie with her new next-door neighbor.

"You're 1B," she whispered.

"Excuse me?"

"The new tenant across the hall in 1B."

He slowly nodded. "Yeah. I moved in today. And, uh, am I to understand that you're 1A?"

"Yes."

He hesitated a long moment.

"Well, uh…nice to meet you?"

The guy had just been kneeling face-level with her—fortunately neatly trimmed—va-jay-jay and all he could manage was *nice to meet you?* Where the hell was the *sorry I was creeping in your closet and spying on you naked?*

"Seriously? That's all you've got?"

A slow, lazy grin tugged at his lips and he glanced down at her robe-covered body. "Uh, *really* nice to meet you?"

She reached for the vase again.

He held a hand up, palm out. "Sorry. But, I mean, you gotta admit, that first meeting is going to be hard to top." He glanced at her thong, still lying on the floor between them. His stare grew a little more heated. "Not to mention bottom."

She growled. Literally. "Just how long were you watching?"

"Long enough to wonder if you're dating a eunuch."

"What?"

"Hey, only a guy with no balls wouldn't like the way you looked in that thong."

Her face reddened and she was torn between thanking him or kicking him. Not only had he seen her—lots of her—but he'd obviously heard her talking to herself. Hopefully he hadn't arrived in time to hear her ask the pretend Dimitri in the mirror if he was into anything naughty and kinky.

Hmm. Wonder if 1B is?

She swallowed the lump in her throat, wishing her brain would stop tossing out these sexy curveballs. She was on the straight-and-narrow, nice-guy-and-a-future path, please-her-father-and-show-him-she-could-do-his-job path. She didn't need any distractions, physically or mentally.

"What were you doing, anyway? Going through your underwear wardrobe, trying to figure out what to wear to entice him?"

"That's none of your business."

He ignored her. "Because, honey, just saying *yes* would be enough enticement for any heterosexual guy on the planet."

Pleasure curled in her when she noted his sincerity. But she crushed it out, remembering she didn't like this man who'd spied on her and gotten two eyes full of her private parts. Not to mention she'd sworn off hot men and this one was so on fire he should have a smoke detector strapped around his chest.

Offering her a sheepish grin, he added, "Look, I'm really sorry I spied on you. I wasn't there for more than a minute. To be honest, I was caught off guard. I just didn't know what to do."

"Going back out the way you came in would have been good."

"I thought this was *my* apartment. But I was going to leave anyway. Then I, uh, opened my eyes and saw you drop your pants."

He'd closed his eyes? Cute.

Well, cute until she thought about what he'd opened them to see. She glanced down at her thong, lying there between them, a small green circle that looked like a Go sign. Grabbing at the flimsy material with her toes, she yanked back the thong, hiding it beneath the folds of her robe.

His lips twitched.

"And instead of leaving, you decided to introduce yourself?" she snapped, more flustered than before.

"Instinct. I just wanted to stop you."

"From doing what? Changing my underwear?"

"I thought you were in my bedroom, remember?"

"Okay, still, what was the big emergency? Were you afraid I was going to leap on your bed and roll around naked, and you wanted to make sure I didn't dirty your sheets?"

That image hit both of them, her words hanging there in the empty air. She suddenly pictured rolling around in the sheets with this man, getting hot, sweaty, dirty. Doing all kinds of wild things that had never even crossed her mind when she'd begun planning a seduction for tonight. Because, deep down, when she'd voiced that pretty/sexy/kinky question to the invisible Dimitri, she'd already known the answer—pretty. Soft, sweet and romantic, that was Dimitri's style. He was a missionary guy all the way, she'd bet her last dollar on it.

One B? Well, he looked like he'd be up for about anything.

It all came back to that camel-in-the-desert question—was she looking for a canteen or an oasis?

She breathed deeper, willing her heart to slow down. It wasn't as if she could lie down and drink from the delicious waters of this particular oasis—she didn't even know this guy!

He, meanwhile, lifted a hand and rubbed his lightly grizzled jaw. She heard the faint rasp of it and suddenly had the image of those unshaven cheeks brushing against her skin. His eyes gleamed as he glanced at her bed—prettily rumpled, the comforter turned down, the pink sheets soft and inviting. She trembled, remembering that ten minutes ago she'd been imagining asking Dimitri to share that bed. Right now, though, she was practically thinking, *Dimitri? Who's Dimitri?*

"I wasn't really thinking," he finally admitted. "I guess I just didn't want to be the kind of guy who'd watch something like that and then skulk away like some kind of pervert."

"So you lunge out and terrify me instead?"

"You didn't look that terrified, and I didn't lunge."

"I was scared to death, and that was some serious lunging."

"I had my hands up to try to block the view."

"You should have watched where you were going,

then maybe you wouldn't have tripped and landed at my feet."

Those lips quirked into a grin. "My intentions were good."

"The results weren't."

"Says you." He shrugged. "Hey, there are only so many things I can apologize for, and landing at the feet of a beautiful, nearly naked woman ain't one of them."

He was staring again. Not at the bed this time, but at *her.* His dark eyes traveled from her bare throat, down to the V in her robe, then farther. As if he liked what he'd seen, and wanted to see a whole lot more.

She reached out and grabbed the edge of her dresser, willing her legs to stop shaking.

"Did I really terrify you?" he asked, his voice lowering to a thick whisper. "I *am* sorry about that."

"My heart's still racing," she admitted.

He didn't ask her to evaluate whether that thumping in her chest was caused by fear...or something else. She didn't ask herself to, either.

"Well, you came across as anything but frightened," he told her, eyeing the vase. "I thought you were going to brain me."

"It was a close call."

"What stopped you?"

"Your bare chest."

Oh, crap, had she really said that?

Laughter burst from him. "So you can notice I'm not wearing a shirt, but I'm not allowed to notice your lack of underpants?"

Her eyes narrowed. "I think you have to agree that

pantsless woman trumps shirtless man in terms of intimate exposure."

"I'll give you that."

How magnanimous. "And I meant," she clarified, "I saw you outside with Anna. You were hard to miss, with no shirt and no shoes. You two looked friendly, so I figured you must know her."

"Gotcha," he said. Then he turned to face the closet. "I obviously misheard our landlady's directions. I could have *sworn* she told me to come through the screen porch and take the door on the left." He frowned. "Actually, at first, I thought I heard her say the right one, then she definitely said left. So maybe she was the confused one."

Or maybe not. Mimi considered the prophetic statement Anna had made a little while ago about a half-naked man tripping at her feet. It was as if she'd known this jeans-wearing three-alarm fire in human form would emerge into her bedroom, trip and land on the floor before her. It couldn't have worked out better if Anna had been there to stick her foot in his path to make him fall.

Aside from being a landlady, Anna also sometimes did some fortune-telling. She read tarot cards and tea leaves, operating out of a local mystic's shop, doing readings under the name Madame Titania. Mimi had always considered it just good fun, nothing really "woo-woo" about it. Now, though… Well, it was interesting, to say the least.

Whether she'd seen something in Mimi's future or not, Anna was probably doing some matchmaking, and had intentionally given 1B the wrong directions. She just hadn't realized that her new tenant wouldn't be the only one half-naked. Though, to be honest, Mimi had been more than half. She'd been three quarters of the way there.

Maybe seven eighths.

She took some small comfort in the fact that she'd still been wearing a bra when he'd seen her. She just wished that if she'd only been allowed to have on one piece of clothing when he'd stumbled in on her, it would have been the damn robe.

"Anna might have gotten a little turned around," she said, not wanting to speculate to this stranger about their landlady's motives. That would open up other questions—like why Anna felt the need to matchmake for her when Mimi had a date standing out in the backyard, probably wondering what on earth had happened to her. A date she was planning to have sex with tonight.

Wasn't she?

"Hey, I just remembered, we haven't been introduced," he said, sticking out his hand. "I'm Xander McKinley."

Not introduced. Right. He'd seen her bare, uh, *everything,* and she'd almost crushed his skull with a vase. But they hadn't exchanged names.

She stared at his hand for a moment, struck by its strength, which matched the strong, bare arm. And the strong, bare shoulders. And the strong, bare chest. Below which was a rippled, bare stomach, covered with a light sprinkling of dark hair that wound down into the waistband of his low-slung jeans.

The man must have lived a previous life and known Webster, because he'd surely provided the definition of *sexy. Hottie,* Anna had called him? What a ridiculous word. He was a flaming inferno.

And wrong. Wrong guy. Wrong time. Wrong situation. Good grief, he'd practically face-planted himself into her naked crotch and wasn't the least bit repentant about it.

He's flirtatious. He's charming. He's a bad boy. He's your next-door neighbor. He's freaking off-limits.

Keeping that in mind, she thrust her hand out, stiff and businesslike. "Mimi Burdette."

She took his hand in hers, noting its calloused, masculine strength. Dimitri was well-built, but his body was the working-rich-man-goes-to-the-gym-four-times-a-week variety. He worked in an office and lifted nothing more than a pen most of the time. He had staff to cut his lawn and a shop to fix his car and hands that proved it.

She shivered. Literally shivered at the thought of this stranger brushing that rough palm and those fingers over all the parts of her he'd already touched with his eyes.

She yanked her hand away. Somebody else was supposed to be touching her tonight. Somebody right. Somebody well-suited for her life and her job and her family. And her.

This guy wasn't him.

"I really need to get back to the party," she said.

He eyed her for a moment, saying nothing, as if he, too, had experienced something strange the moment their fingers had touched. Heck, what *hadn't* been strange about them so far? This whole encounter was already beginning to feel surreal and she wondered if, someday in the future, she'd believe it had been some weird dream.

Not if he's living right under your nose from now on. She was going to be reminded of his hotness and her nakedness every time she bumped into him while getting the mail or carrying in the groceries. Fun times ahead. Only, not.

"The dude…the one who's brainless enough not to like your thong. Is he outside right now?"

She bit her bottom lip, then slowly nodded.

"You're not sleeping with him, though."

"Do we have to repeat that it's-none-of-your-business part of this conversation?"

One corner of his mouth lifted and a twinkle appeared in those deep, dark eyes. "Hey, I feel like I know you intimately already."

True. He knew her almost as intimately as her gynecologist.

"It's not very gentlemanly of you to remind me of that."

He ignored her. "So you and this guy…it's not serious, right? Anna told me you weren't involved with anyone."

Her jaw fell. "You discussed my love life with Anna?"

His turn to flush a little. He looked away, as if wishing he hadn't revealed that much. "Just in passing."

Interesting. Had he asked about her, noticed her outside, the way she'd noticed him?

It doesn't matter.

Still, something made her admit, "It's not serious. Yet."

"But tonight's his lucky night, huh?"

She swallowed, suddenly unsure of that. Unsure of everything.

One B—*Xander, his name is Xander, and how sexy is that?*—stepped closer. "Can I just say, if you've got to work so hard at it, maybe it's just not *supposed* to happen?"

Her mouth went dry as the warmth of his body washed over her. She could smell his skin—a mix of soap and sweat and male—and breathed a little deeper. "Work at it?" she whispered.

He lifted a hand, tracing his fingertip down her cheek, until it rested on the corner of her mouth. "If he wants you badly enough, you could be wearing a nun's habit and he'd still have refused to let you walk into the house without coming after you to try to get you alone."

Ooh. That was so much like what she'd thought earlier, she wondered if he'd read her mind.

"If it were me, I wouldn't have *let* you out of my sight."

She swallowed hard, heat slamming into her, both at his words and the serious, almost dangerous way he'd said them.

"I would have had to stay right beside you throughout the party, just to reassure myself you weren't going to disappear. To make sure no other man even dared to look at you, and to remind myself that I could wait, because, by the time the night was over, you'd be mine."

"Good Lord," she whispered, her eyes falling closed. Her feet shifted; she edged a tiny bit closer, feeling almost mesmerized by his throaty voice. Not to mention by the faint brush of his hand on her mouth. "Really?"

"Oh, yeah," he said. That hand moved, until he was cupping her head, his fingers tangling in her loose hair. She arched her face into his palm, unable to resist, turning to him the way a flower turned to the morning sun. "If I *had* been crazy enough to let you go inside without me, I would have been watching your door, counting down the seconds until you got back. And you can bet your last dollar I would have done something about it if some strange, shirtless dude walked through it after you."

His words held an accusation, but she was too stunned by the feelings rolling through her to launch any kind of defense of Dimitri. Right now, she was finding it hard to concentrate on anything except his scent and his warmth and oh, heavens, the way he was stroking her cheekbone with the side of his thumb.

She opened her eyes, staring at him, realizing she'd already memorized his face, his eyes, his mouth. This stranger was already imprinted on her brain.

"What would you have done?" she whispered. She leaned closer, her body swaying almost against her own will.

"I would have made sure you knew who you were ending the night with." He moved closer, inching toward her. "I would have made you forget any other man existed."

Another inch, then he did it. He covered her mouth with his and made her forget every other man existed.

Shocked at first, Mimi froze for a second, then melted under an onslaught of pure fire. He licked her lips, demanding she part them, and she did, not questioning it. Their tongues met, exploring, hot and wet and hungry. There was nothing polite about this kiss, nothing rehearsed or restrained. He didn't delicately taste her; he devoured her, as if he hadn't eaten in a week and she was his ultimate dessert.

Time, space and reality were lost. Mimi was riding a wave of pure, sultry instinct, every one of her senses humming, all of her nerve endings jangling against his big, rock-hard body. The air she breathed, he provided. She stayed upright only because she had him to lean against. Every delicious flavor she'd ever tasted seemed concentrated in his mouth and she started to shake as they all flooded into her.

Even as a tiny voice inside her tried to remind her he was a stranger, and that she should stop this, she lifted her arms, twining them around his neck. Tangling her fingers in his dark hair, she held on tight, instinctively wanting to make sure he didn't go anywhere. Not before he satisfied this deep, carnal urge she had to be kissed the way every woman ought to be kissed every so often—like she was the sustenance for a man's very soul.

Nobody had kissed her like this. Not ever. Not even men who'd been buried inside her at the time.

"Xander," she groaned against his mouth when he started to pull away.

Hearing his name on her lips seemed to inflame him, because he dove back in again, his tongue plunging deep. He dropped his hands to her hips, claiming her, tugging her even harder against him. When he cupped her bottom, she sighed into his mouth, arching against the delicious, unmistakable ridge of heat pressing against her groin.

He wanted her, there was no denying it, and he wasn't making any effort to keep her from realizing that.

Quivering, almost crying, Mimi pressed harder against him, needing that strength, that pressure. She barely knew him, but she knew she wanted that power, that thickness. All the long pep talks she'd given to herself about being sensible and not needing this kind of heat, this much passion, evaporated and she knew she would do just about anything to have him.

And then it ended, just as abruptly as it had begun. He drew his mouth away from hers, dropped his hands and took a step back. Mimi swallowed hard, trying to regain control of her heart and her lungs, which seemed to be grasping for air.

After a long moment, he nodded. "Yeah, I definitely would have followed you," he said, sounding a little breathless, which told her he, too, was affected by the kiss. "But that's me."

Reality finally started to sink back in. "What… how…you *kissed* me."

"Glad you noticed."

Noticed? Good grief, he'd made the earth rattle beneath her feet.

He turned away from her. "Now, I should go so you can get back to your party."

The floor seemed to lurch, her mind spinning with it. It took a few seconds for her to process the quick change in mood and tone. From flirtatious, to tender to hot-and-kissing? Now to something like…disinterest. *What the ever-loving hell?*

He, on the other hand, seemed just fine. His smile was cheery, that twinkle had reappeared in his eyes. As if he was completely unfazed by their closeness and that amazing kiss, which had affected her clear down to her toenails. No, to the polish on her toenails!

"I guess I'll go try this key on the other door," he said, turning back toward the closet. "Maybe I'll see you later at the party. I told Anna I'd come out."

Still stunned, it took her a few seconds to grasp his words. Once her heart started to beat normally and her brain cells were firing again, she realized she did not want him coming out to that party. She didn't like how easily he'd shown her how receptive she was to him. Especially since she hadn't yet determined whether or not she was receptive to her date, who was waiting for her outside.

But it wasn't exactly polite to order him to stay home until he forgot he'd seen her curl-covered hoo-ha. Or until she'd gotten over that kiss.

"By the way, what'd you decide?" he asked as he ducked into the closet.

"About what?"

He waggled his brows. "The thong? A nice bustier's always a good choice."

Glaring, she reached for the vase.

"Kidding," he said, raising a defensive hand. With a smile that was positively wicked, he added, "Because you're not gonna go through with it."

"Says who?"

"Says the guy who just kissed you…the one you kissed back."

He definitely had her there; she didn't really have a response for that.

He dropped his attention to her lips, then looked

down at her body, her thin robe, her nipples puckering beneath the fabric. He raked his way down the rest of her, to the tips of her toes, before going back up. Then, his voice dropped to a low growl. "Says the guy who loved how you looked in that thong and who really hopes to see it again sometime…caught between something other than your toes."

She gulped, swallowing down a tiny, helpless moan. Because while she had never been the kind of woman who wanted a man to take her for granted, his self-confidence, his certainty of her—what she wanted, how far she'd go—was an incredible turn-on.

With one more smile, he disappeared into her closet. She heard a thump or two as he worked his way back toward the door. Right before he exited, she heard one more thing—his laughing voice.

"By the way, in case you want to know *my* preference, I vote for commando!"

3

WHILE XANDER HADN'T been looking forward to attending the party with a bunch of strangers before meeting his new next-door neighbor, now he could hardly wait. After all his determination to steer clear of Mimi Burdette, the wealthy heiress, now he could think of her only as the girl who dropped her panties—the girl whose mouth tasted like sin and satisfaction—and wanted to see her again.

He must have a masochistic streak. Because, as cocky as his taunting final words to her had been, for all he knew, she was already handing her date a condom and telling him where he could touch her that would make her howl like a she-wolf.

Hmm. Xander didn't want to be told that. He wanted to explore until he found that spot himself.

He wanted her. Badly. He'd wanted her before he'd kissed her, and that kiss had been the X-factor that rocketed want into the stratosphere of bone-shaking desire.

He was going to have a tough time hiding that fact, which meant the wise thing to do would be to stay home. Stay away from the party, and especially stay away from Mimi. She had a date—for tonight at least. And she wasn't his type. He'd figured that out before they even met. She was rich and spoiled and used to getting her own way. He was down-to-earth, and nearly broke after laying out money for first and last months' rent, plus a security deposit. All around a bad combination.

Unfortunately, all those reasonable excuses weren't working. He couldn't get her out of his head.

Nor, he realized, did he want to. He'd already figured out that there was a lot more to her than the pretty, rich-girl package—and he didn't mean just the grade-A ass, lickable thighs and oh-so-delectable everything else. She was funny, sharp, smart. Wrong for him in some ways—her being on the verge of going to bed with another dude being one of them. But right in others. So right he was going to have a hard time sleeping tonight without thinking about the softness of her skin and the sweet scent of her hair, and oh, the taste of that mouth, that soft tongue, those succulent lips. *Heaven.*

And belonging to someone else? *Hell.*

Was all the rest of her going to be someone else's, too? He had to know. "So you're going to that party," he told himself. Because the one thing that would guarantee he got no sleep was if he tortured himself all night long wondering if his prediction that she wouldn't go through with seducing her date had been right or wrong.

He needed to know if she was going home alone.

After cleaning up, taking a quick shower and changing into one of the few pair of dress pants and dress shirts he owned, he headed outside. The party had thinned out a little, but even if it hadn't, he would have easily spotted his new neighbor. She had changed back into her green dress. Her hair was smoothed into place…as if he hadn't had it tangled around his fingers forty minutes ago.

She sat at a table with Anna and Anna's husband, who'd insisted on being called Obi-Wan. Obviously the guy was a *Star Wars* fan. A man and woman Anna had pointed out as the engaged couple sat there, too. And standing at the end of the table, behind Mimi, was a tall guy in a suit.

The boyfriend. No doubt about it.

He wished he didn't immediately recognize that the guy was good-looking. Like, totally hetero male-model good-looking. He was well-built, broad-shouldered, masculine. He wore expensive-looking clothes and a half smile that said he owned the attention of every female in the crowd, and knew it.

Damn. He'd been picturing some sexually ambivalent, boring, pasty-faced, middle-aged guy who wouldn't know what to do with a woman like Mimi and therefore didn't grasp the appeal of a thong. Unfortunately, judging by the way this one was resting his hand with casual possessiveness on her shoulder, he knew. He was practically holding a mine sign over her head, and looked like a fourth grader waving around his brand-new Xbox in front of all his less fortunate buddies the day after Christmas.

Xander had no business curling his fingers into fists. None at all. But curl they did.

She's not yours yet, *pal,* he silently told the other man.

Spying him, Anna immediately waved him over. "There you are—and looking so handsome!"

He handed her the key. "Thanks for the rescue."

"I take it you found your way to where you needed to be?" the older woman asked.

The sparkle in her eye made him wonder if he'd gone exactly where she'd wanted him to. Was his landlady playing matchmaker? "Eventually. Getting there was a bit of an adventure."

"Some people around here could use one," she admitted.

Across the table, Mimi watched, silent, but definitely focused on their conversation. She looked back and forth between him and Anna, but didn't appear surprised. So she'd apparently already figured out Anna had intentionally given him the wrong directions. Interesting.

"Everyone, I want you to meet our new resident, Xander McKinley," Anna said.

They made the rounds saying hello, and he congratulated the bride and groom. Then, when his eyes met Mimi's, he murmured, "Of course, Mimi and I have already met." Some spark of wickedness made him want to pierce a tiny bit of air out of the stiff-necked male model still hovering over Mimi's chair. "Did you ever figure out what to do about that problem you were having?"

She shot him a malevolent glare, but quickly forced a smile to her beautiful lips. "All figured out." Her chin going up, she added, "Thanks for that last suggestion you called out. I have a feeling that's definitely going to do the trick."

His last suggestion. *Commando.*

Xander swallowed hard, trying not to think about

how silky that dress must feel against her bare skin. And especially not to think about who she was wearing all that sexy nothingness for.

"Xander?" said the lucky son of a bitch, his smile tight. "What an...*interesting* name."

"Thanks. Yours was *Dimitri,* right?" he replied evenly, letting his emphasis say what he wanted to say. Let the other guy's hypocrisy come through all on its own. Who the hell was he, anyway, the name police?

"Okay, everyone," Anna interjected, cutting through the sudden tension that had erupted between them, "time for our party favors!"

"You shouldn't have," said the bride, Lyssa, a tall, attractive woman who looked like an Amazon. She had a good three inches of height on her groom, who'd been introduced as Duke.

"It's just for fun," Anna said as she reached under the table and retrieved a large, white-lace-covered box. "Everyone gets one. Before you put your hand inside, I want you to think about what you'd most like to know about your life."

She passed the box around. The guests reached in one by one and pulled out plastic-wrapped fortune cookies, reading out the fortunes as they were drawn. One was apparently going to come into some money, another was about to experience high highs and low lows and a third was destined to change the world.

Of course, they all played the standard, sexy fortune-cookie game—adding the words *between the sheets* after the fortune. There was a lot of commentary about the high highs to be had between the sheets, and he found himself laughing along with the group, most of whom were friendly, young professionals. He might be the only blue-collar guy here, and a stranger to them all, but he didn't feel at all an outsider. Southerners just had a gift for making people feel welcome.

When Mimi drew out her fortune—after one more admonishment from Anna to be sure to think about what she wanted—Xander really started getting interested. What, he wondered, did she most want to know about in her life?

Anna was the first to notice there was more than one tiny slip of paper within Mimi's cookie. "Ooh, a double fortune, that's lucky!"

Mimi merely smiled and plucked the paper free, scraping away the crumbs. Drawing them closer, she said, "There are actually three."

The three tiny slips were stuck together, some kind of factory mistake, but Anna oohed and aahed some more. Her husband, Obi-Wan, who'd been pretty quiet tonight and hadn't had much to say to anyone, piped in. "Must have been some hard concentrating you were doing there, Mimi. The universe is definitely trying to answer your question."

"Read them out loud," someone called.

Mimi smiled and opened her mouth to read the first one. But she just as quickly closed it. Her fist closed around the papers and she reached for her glass of wine.

"What's wrong?" asked Dimitri.

"Nothing. It's just silly. Let someone else have a turn."

"Not until you read," Xander insisted, something making him want to know what it was she didn't want to share.

She frowned at him, then quickly looked away. But, as if realizing nobody was going to let her get away with ignoring her fortunes, she finally unclenched her fingers and lifted the slips again. Her voice low, she read the first one.

"'The man of your dreams is always there to catch you when you fall.'"

"Between the sheets," called one tipsy female.

Everyone laughed. Everyone except Mimi. And Xander. And Dimitri. Because the guy might be okay-looking, and he might be rich. But Xander wasn't sure he met the dashing-hero definition. At least, that's what Xander was telling himself.

"Read the next one," said the bride-to-be.

Mimi sighed, took a deep breath, then read. "'The man of your dreams knows what you really want and how you really want it.'"

That one earned some wolf whistles, catcalls and, of course, the obligatory bed reference. Mimi shot a heated glance at her landlady, obviously wondering—as was Xander—if she'd been set up. But he didn't see how she could have been, considering she'd dug the cookie out of a huge box and all the other fortunes read so far had been normal.

The laughter and whispers died pretty quickly this time. Everyone was curious. Because, not only was Mimi's cookie filled with more than one fortune, but they also seemed to be related. And to have a very pointed, deliberate theme.

Dimitri's hand tightened on Mimi's shoulder, and she turned her head to look up at him. They shared a smile that, to everyone at the party, looked tender and romantic. The sort of smile lovers share.

They weren't lovers. Not yet. But hell, every one of these fortunes she was reading seemed to hint they were about to take that step. That shared smile seemed to confirm it.

Some emotion hit him hard in the chest. Xander recognized it immediately: regret. This was the wrong time and place. She'd already made her choice. A day ago, before she'd made up her mind to lure the other guy into bed, maybe Xander would have had a chance with her. Now? It was too damn late.

His mouth tight and his jaw tighter, he began to back away, wanting to exit the party unnoticed. He'd taken his shot—as much of one as he could take, anyway—and recognized the truth. Whatever might have happened between him and Mimi Burdette just wasn't meant to be.

Which meant it was time to go. He would melt out of her night as quietly and stealthily as he'd entered it.

But before he walked through the back door into the house, he heard her announce she was going to read the third fortune. Something made him wait and listen, nearly hidden in the shadows of the house.

Mimi studied the slip in silence. Lifting her eyes, she looked around as if searching for someone. He watched her, unnoticed, unseen, soon to be forgotten. Then, clearing her throat, she read her third and final fortune.

"'The man of your dreams will slip away unless you have the courage to go after him.'"

THE PARTY WOUND DOWN at around midnight. As the minutes ticked by, the lawn emptied, and Dimitri came up to thank Anna and say good-night, Mimi realized something—she'd completely forgotten she had intended to seduce this man tonight. She hadn't just put the thought out of her mind because she couldn't evaluate how she felt about it, but had actually *forgotten* entirely. Which sure didn't say much for how excited she was about the prospect of going to bed with him.

So it was a good thing she wouldn't be.

She just couldn't. Not after that kiss from another man. Not after the hours she'd spent reliving that kiss, to the point where she'd gotten lost in the middle of more than one party conversation.

"Good night. Thank you again," Dimitri said, gracious, as always.

"You're very welcome," Anna replied with a faint smile.

Mimi walked him to the gate, their arms linked, their steps perfectly matched. She'd noticed before that they always fell into step together, an easy synchronicity that spoke of familiarity and comfort. Heck, maybe that was why she wasn't brokenhearted about not going to bed with him tonight. Maybe they were *too* comfortable. Maybe they'd sort of skipped the passion part of a dating relationship, since they worked together, and had been friends for a few months. Maybe they could even take a few steps back and try to find it.

It bore thinking about, anyway. Another night. When she could actually think about anything except the man in her closet and those crazy fortunes everyone at the party had been buzzing about after she'd read them aloud. Everyone *except* the man in her closet. He'd disappeared sometime during the reading without even saying good-night to anyone. She still couldn't understand why.

"I'll see you on Monday?" Dimitri asked.

She sensed he was waiting to see if she wanted to get together this weekend, if she'd suggest they go out tomorrow or Sunday. Why he didn't ask, she had no idea. It was always this way—he never pursued, just let them drift together. She honestly wasn't sure whether it was because he didn't want to presume, or because he didn't want her to take him for granted.

"Fine," she said with a bright smile.

A shadow crossed his face, momentarily, then he pressed a soft, closemouthed kiss to her lips. She held her breath, waiting to see if he'd deepen it. Waiting to see how she'd feel if he did. Waiting for...something.

She got...nothing. He didn't slide his tongue into her mouth, didn't take her in his arms, didn't lift his hand and tangle it in her hair and cup her face and brush his thumb against her cheekbone.

Normally, she would have backed away with a gentle smile. But tonight, driven by some curiosity she couldn't deny, she slipped her arms up around his neck and held him tight. She tilted her head to the side, parting her lips, inviting him to deepen the kiss.

He did, gently sliding his tongue against hers. He lowered his arms to encircle her waist, keeping his hands above her hips.

Mimi concentrated on the taste of his mouth, the softness of his lips, the feel of his lean body against hers. And it felt good, perfectly fine.

But it definitely did not drive her out of her mind with desire. Actually, she realized, the fact that she could analyze this as she stood here with his tongue in her mouth made her realize how completely uninvolved she was in the moment.

Damn.

He ended the kiss and looked down at her, a question on his impossibly handsome face. Mimi looked up at him, thinking about how she had planned to end the night.

It really wasn't hard to make the right decision.

"Good night, Dimitri," she murmured.

"Good night."

A moment later, he was gone.

Racked with disappointment and a hint of confusion, she went back into the yard to finish helping Anna and found her landlady hard at work taking down some lights. Obi-Wan was with her, doing the same thing, holding the other end. But they weren't even looking at each other, much less talking.

She really wished they would make up. This silent treatment thing was getting ridiculous.

"Thank you so much for your help, dear," said Anna. "Would you do me one more favor and ask my husband if he remembered to shut off the generator in the shed?"

Mimi rolled her eyes, then turned to Obi-Wan. "Did you remember to shut off the generator?"

He smiled and pinched her cheek. "Of course I did. So please tell my darling wife she's not going to get lucky enough to have me inhale noxious fumes and die just yet."

"Oh, for heaven's sake!" Mimi snapped.

They ignored her outburst—and each other—for the next hour as the yard returned to its normal state. As they finished up and entered the screen porch, Obi-Wan stretched and yawned. "I'm going to sleep well tonight, that's for sure. Good thing I have that great big bed to roll around in."

The bed was an issue between them. Anna was sleeping in a twin in the other unit. Anna glared at her husband, then kissed Mimi on the cheek and headed for the door. Once she was gone, Obi-Wan's bright smile faded.

"When are you going to make this right?" Mimi asked, knowing he was miserable without his wife by his side.

"When she gives up that boy toy of hers."

Mimi snorted. Anna would never in a million years cheat.

"It's true! She's always at that theater with that jerk."

"She's doing costumes for Shakespeare in the Park."

"Fred Phelps doesn't need one. He's always looked like he has an ass's head anyway. To think I once golfed with the man!"

"You really need to let this go."

He put a hand up, stopping her from saying anything more. A peace lover he might be, but he was also incredibly stubborn. The subject was closed.

"I think I'll go to bed, too. You sleep well."

"I doubt I'll do that," she admitted as they went inside the large common area on the bottom floor that separated her apartment from Xander's.

"Why not? You must be so tired."

"You'd think so. Unfortunately, I'm too keyed up to sleep."

That was true; she felt wired, on edge. She suspected sleep would be a long time coming tonight, probably because her head was too filled with fortunes and closets and thongs and big, broad-shouldered, bare-chested men.

"I've got just the thing," said Obi-Wan, reaching into a pocket of his voluminous shirt. "Have some of my special tea."

She eyed the pouch dubiously. "Uh…I don't think so."

"Nothing illicit, I promise," he insisted, raising a hand to make a Scout's pledge. She doubted he'd ever been a Scout, however—too militaristic for this peacenik. "Just some herbs and spices. You'll sleep like a baby and have pleasant dreams."

"I rarely dream."

He smirked. "That's not what that fortune cookie said."

"Don't remind me." That had been so embarrassing, having to read those fortunes, as if she'd really been thinking about nothing else but the man of her dreams. As if she didn't have a stressful job, problems with her father, a friend's wedding to help plan. The man of her dreams was the last thing on her mind.

Sex? Well, that wasn't the last thing on her mind, but her fortunes hadn't been just about sex. They'd also been about romance and love—at least that's how everyone had interpreted them. She didn't have time for any of that, which was why her relationship with Dimitri seemed so ideal. She could get the sex and possibly even the relationship without dealing with the other stuff—and the heartache that often went along with it.

So why can't you stop thinking about your new neighbor?

Good question.

"I promise, this will relax you and you'll wake up in the morning feeling clearheaded and full of energy."

"No magic mushrooms?" she asked, still suspicious.

"Cross my heart."

He slipped the packet of tea into her hand and said good-night. She watched him go up the stairs to his apartment, then went to her own front door. With one last, lingering glance at the closed one across the hall, she went inside.

Sighing in renewed embarrassment as she saw the balled-up thong on the floor of her room, she stripped out of her dress—beneath which she *was* wearing underwear, albeit plain white satin ones—and got ready for sleep.

She didn't really intend to drink Obi-Wan's special blend, but after lying in bed for an hour, tossing and turning as she'd predicted, she got up and put the kettle on. She sniffed as the tea brewed, not noticing anything too out of the ordinary. Definitely spices, sweet and tangy. She caught cinnamon and nutmeg, maybe some orange? It seemed innocent enough, and she suddenly found herself wanting to taste it.

"Okay, Obi-Wan, I'm trusting you," she said as she lifted the cup. "If there's wacky weed in here, you're in trouble."

A bevy of fragrances filled her nose, and she sighed in pleasure as the liquid hit her tongue. The brew tasted like no tea she'd ever consumed, and she savored each heavenly sip as she headed back for her bedroom. The steam cleared her nose and the flavors awakened her taste buds. For a second, she felt more wide-awake, in tune with her senses, from the feel of the hardwood floor beneath her feet, to the faint, lingering man-smell in her bedroom. *Oh, that's* really *delicious.*

Then a languor swept over her. Her muscles relaxed, the drumming of her pulse in her temple diminished. She almost purred as she slipped back into the bed, remaining upright to finish the tea down to the very last drop. Her lips and tongue were tingling and the taste lingered for a long time after she'd taken her final sip.

"Obi-Wan," she mumbled as lovely warmth drenched her entire body, "you should package this stuff and sell it retail."

It wasn't just delicious, it was every bit as relaxing as he'd promised. She was practically asleep before her head hit the pillow, and once it did, she was out like a light.

And dreaming…

It was early morning. The sky was so blue and sharp it almost hurt to look at it, and the air felt cold and crisp in Mimi's lungs. She wondered if this could still be Georgia, and immediately doubted it. She couldn't say where she was—the colors were all so vivid, the earth so alive. She didn't recognize such vibrancy, she only knew she'd never seen it before.

She was barefoot, walking in dew-drenched grass across a lush lawn. Nearby, a warm house beckoned. No, not a house—a palace, with high turrets, arched windows, gables and cupolas. The top story was swathed in mist and it looked almost like a castle from a fairy tale. It promised wealth and security.

"Come back!" called a voice from within. It commanded obedience, expected it.

She hesitated for a moment, but in the end, did not turn back. She was instead drawn farther away, toward a stand of dark, shadowy woods that stood just outside the manicured castle lawn. Mysterious and magical, maybe a bit frightening; she couldn't resist the silent allure of the dark, twisting trees.

As she stepped into the forest, she was surprised to find the air had grown warmer. The ground was soft, gentle against her bare toes. She drew deep breaths into her lungs, drawn to some unseen source of heat, feeling excited, half-wondering if she should stop, but knowing she wouldn't.

She walked on, hearing the crunch of leaves beneath her feet, pulled irresistibly forward by some invisible force of nature that drew her ever onward. That peaceful feeling slowly began to evaporate and tension built within her, though she couldn't say why.

The ground gained heat somehow and the forest fell quiet. So very quiet. And the air was now almost too hot to suck into her mouth. Sweat broke out on her brow.

Her steps slowed. She turned and looked over her shoulder, toward the castle, but could barely make out its outline as the woods seemed to have swallowed her whole.

She told herself she should go back, but her feet wouldn't let her turn around. The air gained mass, growing thick, blocking her from moving any way but forward.

Suddenly, she reached a clearing and came face-to-face with a dark mountain. A large cave was cut into its side, and something within that cave was breathing loudly. Each breath filled the day, consumed all other sound, sucked away thought.

Filled with terror, she froze in place. Heat assaulted her; she couldn't think, could barely breathe.

The loud form moved to the entrance of the cave. She saw an enormous head, then a slowly unfurling wing, green and scaly.

A dragon.

It opened its mouth and sparks flickered between its jagged teeth. She screamed and turned to run, only instead of seeing the woods, she was horrified to realize she now stood at the edge of an enormous cliff. A thousand feet below was a jagged beach, with raging waters and vicious rocks. She was caught between the fire of the dragon's mouth and an anguished fall to her death.

Pebbles shifted beneath her feet. The ground gave way. She began to fall.

"Hold on, I've got you!" a voice suddenly called.

She looked up and saw a figure swooping down from the mountain above her, dressed all in black, from head to toe. His features were disguised by a mask that covered his whole face.

"The dragon!" she shrieked.

"Trust me."

He grabbed her around the waist, swinging them both out over the cliff's edge. The dragon nipped at their toes and she looked down and saw a watery grave far below. But the masked man held her tight against his massive chest, as if she weighed nothing. She felt safe, completely protected, yet also energized and so very free.

All at once, they weren't swinging on a rope—they were flying. Together, they soared through the sky, over the ocean, past the forest, beyond the castle. Right into the horizon.

"You rescued me from the dragon," she finally whispered, her arms curled around his shoulders, her face pressed into his neck.

"No. I rescued you from a dull, safe, predictable life in that boring castle,*" he replied.*

She didn't understand how he could know that, or even if it was true. But right now, it didn't matter. She was content to lose herself in the feel of his strong body as they flew and flew, certain that nothing could ever make them return to the ordinary land below.

4

Having arranged his move-in around his shift-work at the station, Xander had the entire weekend to finish unpacking his apartment. He had sold most of his stuff—along with his parents' things—in Chicago. So there wasn't much to move aside from his clothes. He'd ordered new furniture, which had been delivered the previous day. Beyond putting personal stuff away, there wasn't a lot to do. By Sunday afternoon, he was completely finished.

Remembering his landlady had asked him to hold on to his moving boxes, since tenants often needed them, he decided to take them outside to the free-standing garage. He'd just finished flattening them and standing them in the corner when he heard the clanging of metal from somewhere outside.

Curious, he walked around the building, looking toward the woods that backed up to the old house. He immediately spied a metal ladder propped up against an enormous, flower-covered tree. A sneaker-clad foot disappeared up that ladder, its owner swallowed up in the profusion of low-hanging limbs and branches.

"Bad move," he muttered, tsking as he noted the unsteadiness of the ground on which the extension ladder stood. It was leaning against a gnarled, uneven tree trunk, and the person using it had climbed far too high for someone to go without having any support at the base.

Jogging over, he called, "Hey, let me spot you!"

He reached the ladder and braced it, tightly gripping both sides and planting a foot against the bottom rung. When he finally glanced up, he saw two feet, above which were two long, slim legs and a curvy set of hips.

He'd recognize this view anywhere. Clothed or unclothed. As for which he preferred? Well, a gentleman would never tell.

He'd seen Mimi the previous day, but they hadn't said much more than hello. He'd wanted to, badly, especially after what had happened between them in her room. But he hadn't done it.

Needing to know what her decision had been Friday night, he had sat in his living room, going over some paperwork, with his ear cocked. And he'd heard the deep, male voicc mingling with her sweet, sultry tones in the vestibule between their apartments. More importantly, he had not heard the distinctive squeak of the front door to the house—meaning her friend had not left. So it hadn't been hard to figure out she had, indeed, invited her potential lover into her home. And her bed. Which had reconfirmed his decision to steer clear of his beautiful neighbor.

Now, though, he couldn't exactly steer clear when she was being so reckless up on that unsecured ladder.

"How's it going, neighbor?"

"Xander?" she called. "What are you doing?"

"You shouldn't climb so high without someone supporting the ladder."

"I know," she said, sounding sheepish. "I just wanted to get some fresh magnolias. I love them—they're my favorite flower. They make the house smell so nice. But the ones on the ground are all brown, and we picked the ones near the bottom for the party."

"Okay, keep going, I'll hold on until you've finished."

"Thanks, I appreciate it."

He kept his head tilted back, watching her through the leaves and shadowy branches. Telling himself he just wanted to make sure she didn't slip, he pretended he wasn't appreciating every inch of those long, bared legs.

"Oh, God!"

"What's wrong?"

"It's a bee's nest," she said with a soft, worried groan.

"Calm down. Don't panic." He tightened his grip on the ladder, stepping to the side and trying to see up to the fork in the branches at which she was staring. "Start climbing down."

She didn't move.

"Mimi, come on, just back down one rung at a time. If you don't bother them, they shouldn't bother you."

"I'm allergic," she whispered. "Seriously allergic, and I don't have an EpiPen with me."

"It's going to be fine," he insisted, despite the fact that his tension had skyrocketed when she revealed how serious the allergy was. If she needed epinephrine, it was bad. "Just move one foot down. Come on, you can do it." He would go up to her but no way would he risk both their weights on an unsecured ladder. "One step at a time. Right down here to me, piece of cake."

She moved down one rung, not looking where she was going, never taking her eyes off what appeared from here to be a nest as big as her face. Her second foot came down and met the first one on the rung, then she slowly moved down one more.

"That's right, nice and easy," he insisted.

She nodded and made it down one more. Then, from another branch, something buzzed up and swooped near her head. From here, it looked like a dragonfly. He imagined in her frightened, allergic mind, she was seeing the world's most ginormous bee.

"No!" she snapped, waving a hand at it.

"Don't let go…."

Too late. She lost her grip. Trying to grab hold of the rung again, she yelped as it slipped through her fingers.

She fell.

Xander's blood roared in his veins, but he reacted instinctively. Letting go of the ladder, he stepped back and extended his arms. As she plunged toward the ground, he caught her and swooped her out from under the tree. Behind them came the bees, whose nest had been disturbed by the jerking ladder.

"Hold on," he ordered. Holding her close, he darted around the garage and ducked inside. The cloud of buzzing, angry bees followed, but kept right on going out toward the street.

They stood there in the shadows of the musty garage, sucking in deep, ragged breaths. It had all happened in probably no more than sixty seconds, but it had felt longer in his mind.

Xander didn't put her down, holding her tightly against his body, one arm under her bent knees, the other her shoulders. He couldn't stop thinking about how it could have gone down. Couldn't get the image out of his mind, visualizing the way she'd looked as she'd crashed backward from so high up.

Even worse, his imagination filled in the blanks of what might have happened had he not been there. He practically heard the crunch of her body as she landed flat on her back on the hard ground. Could almost see the swarm of bees attacking her. And knew enough about bee allergies to know she could have been in very serious trouble if enough of them had gotten her.

Jesus. All for a couple of flowers, one of which she still had crushed to her chest.

Finally feeling as though he'd managed to bring his heart rate and his breathing under control, he looked at her face. She was pink-cheeked, wide-eyed. Her hair was tangled around her face, and a scratch marred one cheek. Her lips were parted and trembling and he saw the way her throat worked as she swallowed.

Finally, she whispered, "You saved me."

Their stares met and locked. Heat and intensity flared up between them, as powerful as it had been Friday night. No, more so, because this time, they were wrapped together, her soft body pressed against his, her beautiful face so kissably close.

He thought about it. Seriously considered kissing the lips right off her, if only as a close-call reaction. But in the end, remembering her boyfriend—the one she had obviously slept with judging by that male voice he'd heard in the hallway—he squashed the impulse.

He could forgive himself for one stolen kiss when she hadn't been seriously involved with anyone. Now he knew she was.

"Yeah. Saved you from the big, bad dragonfly."

She scrunched her nose. "Is that what it was?"

"I think so," he said, slowly lowering her to the ground.

She swiped a hand through her hair. Xander reached out and plucked a few leaves from the long red strands, allowing himself a brief moment of pleasure at the soft feel of the curls against his fingertips.

"I still can't believe I fell off that ladder and you caught me," she said.

"Forget it," he said. "Me and ladders go way back."

"Can I…offer you a beer or something as a thank-you?"

He thought about it, considered the boyfriend. He shouldn't, really. It had been hard enough to try not to think about her after Friday night. Why add to his stockpile of Mimi moments when nothing could come of them?

But some inner masochist answered. "Sure, that'd be great."

She offered him a smile, then reached up and smoothed her hair back, tucking it behind her ears. "Why don't we sit out on the patio? Do you think the coast is clear?"

"The bees?"

"Uh-huh."

He stuck his head out and peered around the side of the garage, toward the backyard. The ladder on which she'd been standing was now lying on the lawn. He'd been so pumped up with adrenaline he hadn't even heard it falling after her. He winced as another mental image shot to mind—of her on the ground and that huge thing landing on her.

She should never have been out there, hauling that ladder around, then climbing it, without any help whatsoever. He couldn't help wondering where Mr. Perfect was and why he hadn't been here for his girlfriend.

"All clear," he said, forcing away the protective instincts. She was his neighbor, nothing else. They could be…neighborly. Have a beer. Share ten minutes of sunshine on a Sunday afternoon. No kissing. No thongs. No lusting.

No way.

It was crazy to even think he'd be able to manage that. He opened his mouth to say he'd changed his mind. But before he could, she gave him a bright smile. "Okay, I'll go get the beer and meet you on the patio?"

He was helpless against that smile. "Fine."

Watching her go, he was very aware of the sway of her hips and backside. He shook his head, trying to remind himself she was being friendly, just showing a little appreciation because he'd helped her out. He needed to forget everything else beyond that. Especially the way she'd looked *out* of those shorts.

His jeans suddenly tightened as that image forced itself to the forefront of his mind.

He attempted to tamp down the reaction by shifting his thoughts to less appealing things—like grits, God in heaven, who had ever decided to eat what looked like little pieces of dandruff? That helped, but he sensed his cock would remain ready to leap to attention until he got Mimi out of his mind and out of his system.

And wasn't that going to be fun considering she lived right next door?

Heading for the patio, he sat down to wait, taking a good, daylight look around his new backyard. There had probably once been a much bigger lawn around the old plantation house, but the Georgia woods had encroached over the years. Now huge live oaks shaded much of it, and the little bit of grass quickly gave way to a carpet of evergreen needles and earth. It smelled like Southern summer, with a mix of peaches and pine, nothing like what he was used to in Chicago.

"Here you go," she said when she returned, handing him an icy-cold bottle dripping with condensation. She'd brought one for herself, too, and twisted the top off it as she sat down.

"Thanks." He opened the beer, sipped deeply, then nodded. "I didn't realize how hot it was out here. Guess I'll have to get used to these Southern summers."

She laughed. "Summer? Are you joking? This is only early June. By August fifteenth, you're going to be calling Hell and asking them to send up some cooler air."

"That bad, huh?"

"Worse. Is this really your first summer in Georgia?"

He sipped the beer again, nodding. "I was born and raised in Chicago. Never even visited south of the Mason-Dixon Line until I came down to interview for my new job here."

"Which is?"

"I'm a firefighter."

Her eyes widened. "That explains the ladder crack."

"Yep."

"So you're used to heat."

More used to it every minute he spent with her. "You could say that. What about you?"

"I'm in sales."

"What do you sell?" He grinned. "Please tell me it's not thongs."

"Ha. I actually run the marketing department for Burdette Foods."

He of course recognized the name. "Family business?"

"Yes. My father's the CEO. What does your family think about you moving so far away from home?"

His jaw clenched for just a moment. He supposed he needed to get used to questions like that, but it was still hard to say the words he forced to his mouth. "I don't have any family."

A frown formed between her eyes. "Oh."

"I'm an only child of two only children," he explained. "And my parents both passed away last year."

She reached across the table and put her hand on his, squeezing briefly. It was obviously an impulsive move, driven purely by kindness, but he reacted to the softness of her touch, his heart flipping over in his chest. Just as he'd reacted to everything about this woman since he'd first heard her voice in her bedroom the other night.

"I'm so sorry."

"Thanks." He thrust off the flash of sadness, explaining, "It had been a rough couple of years, and they made me promise to go do some living once they were gone."

"So you came to Athens, Georgia?" she asked with an amused lift of the eyebrow.

"My Mom was Greek, but I couldn't afford the airfare to the other Athens."

"Greece is on my bucket list."

"Mine, too," he admitted.

"Ever since I saw *Mamma Mia,* I've wanted to see the Greek Isles."

"Ever since I was a kid, I've wanted to go find the person who invented the name Lysander and punch him in the jaw."

They laughed together.

"Lysander? That's your real name? Seriously?"

"Yep." Having been curious since they'd met, he asked, "Tell me what Mimi's short for."

She hesitated.

"Come on, I told you mine, you tell me yours."

Sighing, she mumbled, "Hermione."

"Like in…"

"Don't say it," she snapped, holding a hand up, palm out. "The next person who asks me if I'm named after a character in the Harry Potter books is going to get a slap. I mean, how long can those books have been out? Do I look like a teenager?"

He couldn't resist casting another look over her, from sun-tossed red hair, to beautiful face, slim neck, high breasts pressing against her tank top, all the way down her long, bare legs. *Definitely not a teenager.*

"I wasn't going to suggest you were named after her."

"It's my grandmother's name. I'm an only child, but I have a few cousins. I think my father was angling for a bigger trust fund for me while I was still in the womb."

Trust fund. Ouch. Another reminder that he was so

out of his league with this woman. "How'd that work out for ya?"

Her mouth turned down. "About like he hoped it would."

Interesting. She wasn't happy with her silver spoon. He'd already guessed as much, judging by her lifestyle.

"So if you'rc a superrich trust-fund kid, why are you living in an apartment house and figuring out how to fit three-for-a-buck boxes of macaroni-and-cheese and half-price toilet paper on the same page of a sales circulars?"

"Food and bathroom products on the same page? Never! That's basic freshman marketing."

"Sorry, I never took that class. I was busy with ladder-climbing 101 and fire-hose handling." Seeing her confusion, he chuckled. "Kidding. I never went to college." Seeing a flash of confusion—*or pity? Please God, not pity*—cross her face, he quickly added, "Classic underachiever. That's me."

Joking was better than getting into the subject. By the time he was eighteen, he was working full-time to help his dad pay the bills and take care of his mom, who was five years into an MS diagnosis. There'd been no time for school and certainly no money. But they didn't need to discuss that.

"I somehow doubt it," she said, disbelieving. "It takes a special kind of person to do what you do—putting your life on the line to help others. You're a real hero. Marketers are a dime a dozen."

Uncomfortable with the praise, he asked, "Is that your professional opinion, having analyzed the cost-versus-value-added benefits of marketers?"

She laughed lightly, and he pressed forward with the subject change. He'd made his decision to enter his career for valid reasons, and was proud of what he did. He didn't need anyone else's strokes telling him he'd done the right thing. If he got strokes from this woman, he wanted them to be of a very different variety.

Not happening, dude. Boyfriend, remember?

"So, you never answered my question."

She glanced toward the big house, once white, now more gray after a hundred and fifty years of weather and history. "I love this place. I love living here."

"It is special. But couldn't you buy one just like it?"

She shook her head. "I could probably afford a house, but not like this one. The trust fund's tied up with the family business—I couldn't touch it if I wanted to. And I won't take money from my parents. I work hard for what I earn."

"I always figured there were two kinds of boss's kids. Those who got away with murder, counting on Daddy to bail them out. And those who worked twice as hard as everyone else to try to prove something. Do I have to guess which you are?"

She sank into her chair. "I have to cop to the second."

"I figured."

"I started working in one of the stores as a cashier as soon as I turned sixteen. I've baked cakes, sliced deli meats, stocked shelves, even did some turkey bowling in my day."

He lifted a curious brow.

A tiny dimple appeared in one perfect cheek as she grinned. "The night after Thanksgiving, when the stores were being restocked and a lot of frozen turkeys were left unsold, the stock guys used to set up bowling alleys with stacks of empty containers at one end, and use the birds as the balls."

He snorted a laugh. "Sounds like fun. So I guess you really have worked your way to the top in the family business."

She glanced away, toward the sky, which was turning purple and blue as the sun dropped lower in the sky toward evening. "I don't want what I haven't earned. I was determined to prove to my father that I am not just a useless daughter, good only for patting on the head and sending out to buy dresses."

Ouch. Despite the softness of her pretty, lyrical voice, the pain came through loud and clear. "Daddy issues?"

"I don't need his approval," she snapped. "I want his job when he retires."

And obviously, she was afraid she wasn't going to get it. Or thought there was a chance she might not.

Licking her lips and not meeting his eye, she explained, "I guess that's a bit of a lie. I do want his approval—or at least, I want him to think I want it. He's resisting the idea of a woman taking over the company his grandfather founded, which he almost single-handedly saved from bankruptcy ten years ago." She huffed. "I have an MBA, but I don't have a penis."

Thank God.

"You don't have any siblings," he pointed out, remembering what she'd said earlier.

"Male cousins."

All other things being equal in terms of the job, it seemed crazy to him that any parent would favor a nephew over his own child just because of her sex. Talk about a strange value system. Mimi acted like the only thing that mattered was the job, but he couldn't imagine it was easy growing up and always being made to feel somehow "less" in the eyes of a parent.

His own upbringing had included a lot of struggle, mostly because of his mom's illness, but his parents had always made sure he knew they loved him.

"My cousins aren't even interested in the business—one's a lawyer, one's a pilot, another's a musician."

So, all things weren't equal. And the father was still being sexist? Bizarre.

"So you must really love what he does if you so want his job, huh?"

She thought about it for a moment, then admitted, "No. Not really. I like sales and marketing—honestly, I would rather be trying to sell more than cold cuts and jelly doughnuts."

He laughed. "Then why are you so determined to stick with the grocery biz?"

"I guess I'm just the type who never likes being told I can't do something. Hearing from the time I was a kid that a man had to run the company was like waving a red cape in front of a bull."

"Sorry, but I have to say, your dad sounds like a tool."

She chuckled. "He's all right. Just old-fashioned and stubborn. I haven't exactly made it easy on him."

"What kid does?"

"Well, my mom tells me I always went out of my way to do the opposite of what he suggested. He wanted me to take dance lessons as a little girl—I insisted on karate. He hoped I'd be interested in music in school, I was interested in boys and track. He wanted me to go to Georgia State, I went all Yankee on him, to that evil, great wild north known as Maryland."

"Whatever Daddy says…you go the opposite way."

"In the past," she admitted. "But now, going all Sigmund Freud on myself, I suspect that's why I started going out with Dimitri. To extend an olive branch, do something he wanted for a change. And to make my father think I see things just the way he does. He sees Dimitri as perfect for me."

He tensed. Couldn't help it, his muscles just stiffened reflexively when he heard the other man's name.

The other man? Make that—her lover's name.

"So your boyfriend comes with Daddy's stamp of approval?"

"He's not my boyfriend," she immediately replied.

He couldn't help pushing the issue. "Your lover?"

A long hesitation. Then she admitted, "Not that, either."

His heart skidded. "I thought…I heard voices in the hall late Friday night, after everyone was gone."

She looked down, her lashes hiding those expressive eyes, as if she didn't want him to read too much into her words. "That was Obi-Wan. Dimitri was long gone by then."

"So you didn't…"

"No. We didn't." Like a broken record, she again reminded him, "Not that it's any of your business."

No, of course it wasn't. But that didn't stop him from wanting to fist bump the sky. "Got it."

Their stares met, and he suspected she was reading his silent relief, evaluating it, figuring out how she felt about it. Hell, he didn't know how he felt about it himself. It wasn't as if he had any kind of chance with this woman beyond being friendly, sharing a beer and occasionally saving her ass from bees and falling ladders.

He was also willing to offer underwear advice anytime she required it. Hey, he was neighborly that way.

But anything else? Was that really possible?

A bird landed on a feeder nearby, and a lawn mower started up down the street. But Xander couldn't tear his attention off her face. He found himself trying to figure out whether her eyes were more blue or purple, wondering if he'd ever seen such a vivid shade before and sure he hadn't.

Finally, she looked at her beer bottle, as if the stare had grown too intense. "Speaking of Dimitri, I know he came across as rude at the party. I'm sorry about that name crack."

"You don't need to apologize for him."

"I think he felt some kind of vibe between you and me. I guess I was feeling embarrassed over you walking in on me like you did, and he sensed it. So he was being a little protective."

"Like a kindergartener guarding the last Fruit Roll-Up in the box."

She offered him a cheeky grin. "Fruit Roll-Ups *can* be on the same page as macaroni-and-cheese, by the way."

He smiled, but didn't let her get away with changing the subject again. "You know you don't belong with him."

His bluntness seemed to take her by surprise. "What's wrong with him?"

"Absolutely nothing. That's the problem."

Her brow scrunched in confusion.

"I mean, he's too perfect."

Hearing her tiny gasp, he wondered if that was something she'd been wondering about herself.

"Guys like that usually end up with Barbie dolls on their arms." He cast a quick, rakish look over her body. "And I'm not saying you don't fit the bill in terms of being one hell of a beautiful woman, but you sure aren't made of plastic."

She opened her mouth, then closed it again, as if not sure what to say. Finally, she whispered, "Thanks."

"Dimitri's in over his head with you, and I suspect he knows it. Because as much as you want to make peace with Daddy, I already know there's a lot more to you than the grocery-store sales-circular queen."

"He's not a bad guy," she insisted.

"Maybe not. But he has no idea what to do with *you.*"

"Do with me? You make me sound like I'm some kind of troublesome teenager."

"You're trouble all right," he said with a wry grin. "But you're not the problem. He is. He doesn't know what you want or how to give it to you."

She gasped, and Xander suddenly remembered the second prediction from her fortune cookie the other night. He hadn't meant to echo them, but now that he'd said the words, he couldn't deny he believed them.

"And I'm not adding the words *between the sheets* here," he said, not wanting her to think he was being salacious. "I mean, I would lay cash money Dimitri has no idea how badly you want your father's job, or how much it hurts you that your old man's resisting."

"Well, I…"

"I also bet he isn't happy about you living here and hasn't got a clue why you do."

The tightening of her mouth confirmed that theory.

"And does he have the slightest idea that you go all Katy Perry when you're in the shower?"

Her jaw fell open.

"Thin walls, babe," he told her with a wicked grin.

"Note to self—no more singing 'Last Friday Night' in the shower," she mumbled.

"Don't stop on my account. Did you know you actually got a little louder on the ménage-à-trois line?"

"Shut up," she said, laughing.

He went back to this point. "Anyway, nope, the walking Ken doll doesn't know the real you at all."

"How can you possibly know that?"

He shrugged. "Because he let you walk into that house *alone* to try on fancy underwear Friday night. Meaning he has no idea how badly you need to be…"

"Whoa, there, hold on."

He held up both hands, palms out. "Sorry. I meant, he has no idea how badly you wanted to have sex. Hot, wild, steamy sex. The guy's got no clue."

Her lips parted and she took a long, slow breath. He could practically see the thoughts churning behind her violet eyes and knew he'd been pretty outspoken about something that didn't concern him. Still, he had been thinking about this since Friday night, and now that he'd said something, he couldn't bring himself to regret it.

Of course, he didn't go on. He didn't tell her he suspected that, after their hot kiss, she had been thinking about having hot steamy sex with someone else. As had he.

And considering she'd already admitted she had not started sleeping with another man, he had begun to wonder if he still had a shot with her after all.

Finally, she managed to say, "My relationship with Dimitri is really..."

"None of my business. Yeah, yeah. I know." He leaned back in his chair, kicking his legs out and crossing his feet at the ankle. "Of course, considering you were half-naked and kissing me a few minutes after trying on seduction lingerie meant for him, maybe it is my business."

Her jaw dropped. "You kissed me."

"I didn't feel you resisting." Far, *far* from it.

"You caught me off guard, that's all."

"For five solid minutes?"

"It wasn't five minutes."

"It was at least five minutes. Maybe ten."

"Ten *seconds,* at most."

She looked like she was about to continue, probably to insist his watch was broken and the clock moved backward, and up was down, but he snorted. "Keep telling yourself those lies."

She sputtered, obviously not used to not getting the last word. Finally she went for the third-grader response. "You...you jerk."

"However long it lasted, you've got to admit, that was a hell of a kiss."

She crossed her arms over her chest, keeping her mouth closed, not daring to deny it. Her quivering lips and out-thrust chin looked more adorable than determined.

Adorable…like everything else about Mimi Burdette. She was gorgeous, funny, smart. And oh, so damn stubborn.

He couldn't resist teasing her a bit more. "I'm assuming your housewarming gift for your new neighbors don't always include tongue?"

Fire snapped in her eyes. No more silent treatment. He almost regretted baiting her. "I wasn't your Welcome Wagon. How many times do we have to go over this—you were in *my* apartment. I could have had you arrested as a prowler."

"I bet the cops would have enjoyed the view as much as I did."

The vocabulary went from third-grade to middle-school level.

"You ass!"

When she launched up from the table, he reached out a hand, putting it on hers and entwining their fingers. "Stay."

"Why should I?"

With a simple shrug, he explained, "Because you're not really mad, and you're having fun. Even though you're ready to find a vase to break over my head, you like me."

She hesitated.

"Come on," he cajoled, "when's the last time anybody ever gave you shit and made you laugh at yourself? I suspect you're always serious at work, subduing the real you, wanting to stay on Dad's good side for a change and fit into that world even though you don't always like it. And your un-boyfriend sure didn't look like the life of the party. So hell, Hermione, finish your beer, let your hair down and just enjoy the sunset, why don't you?"

"Don't call me Hermione," she insisted, looking like she couldn't decide whether to slap him or laugh at the entire conversation.

Then she fell silent, standing there, gazing down at him, their hands together. He saw indecision cross her face and knew she was tempted. He also knew he was right—it was a rare thing for this woman to just let herself be silly and relax. She'd made the decision to thrust the free-spirited part of herself away and focus on being the kind of daughter her father wanted.

It was shameful. As far as Xander was concerned, both her father and this Dimitri douche had a lot of explaining to do. Especially for things as simple as the fact that this amazing woman didn't even remember how to unwind on a beautiful evening like this one.

Unable to resist, now that he knew she was technically still single, he pulled her hand closer, lifting it to his lips. He had kissed her mouth Friday night, but hadn't had a chance to explore all that soft, fragrant, feminine skin.

And he wanted to. Badly. Her hand would do for a start.

He pressed a kiss in the fleshy part of her hand, between her thumb and index finger. Hearing her tiny sigh, he kissed again, this time flicking out his tongue to taste her. Her fingers went limp in his, and he freed them to turn her hand over. That gave him her palm to explore, and he began to do it, kissing his way to the life lines in the center.

It was the simplest of kisses, seemingly innocent, but still somehow incredibly personal. Because all he could think about as he tasted her hand was moving on to her wrist, and her arm, and her shoulder and her throat. On, and on and on. There were miles of Mimi to explore, vast, feminine spaces, and doing it out here in the sunshine sounded like his idea of heaven.

"Oh, are we having a B.Y.O.M. cookout?" a voice called, interrupting the moment.

Xander immediately dropped her hand and sat straight up. Obi-Wan was coming out of the house, accompanied by a thin, pale guy Xander had met at the party. He was a tenant on the second floor, a writer, Will…Sherman? Shaker? Something like that.

Mimi walked to them quickly, and he couldn't tell if she was glad for the interruption or was simply embarrassed. "That sounds great," she said. Then she looked back over her shoulder. "Every once in a while everybody raids their fridge and brings out stuff for a community cookout. Bring Your Own Meat." She nibbled her bottom lip, as if undecided, then quickly added, "Why don't you join us?"

It was a house event, so he probably hadn't required the invitation. But he was glad she'd extended it anyway. Very glad. Whatever she'd felt about the things he'd said, or the way he'd kissed her hand, she was willing to keep exploring whatever was happening between them.

Something was happening between them, of that he had no doubt. He couldn't put a name on it, and had no idea where it was going. The only thing he did know was that he and Mimi had been like water put in a pot on a warm burner. Things were heating up. When or if they would come to a boil, he honestly didn't know.

But he sure planned to stick around to find out.

"I'd love to."

5

Mimi had always enjoyed the impromptu backyard cookouts with her neighbors, and this weekend's was no exception. At first, she'd worried about Xander's presence, considering she simply couldn't decide how she felt about the man. In the end, though, she was glad he'd stayed. Very glad.

He was, in truth, incredibly charming. Friendly, funny, easy to talk to. By the end of the night, he'd made her completely forget she was mad at him for taunting her about the way they'd met, and about her relationship with Dimitri. She'd also forgotten she'd promised herself she wasn't going to let herself enjoy being with him.

She couldn't help enjoying his company; nobody could. He was just the kind of man everyone wanted to be around. He helped Obi-Wan with the grill, ran out for ice to fill the cooler for Anna, spent a half hour talking firefighter stuff with Will, who swore he intended to write a character just like Xander in one of his plays.

And he kept murmuring under-the-breath jests to Mimi. Mostly innocent, but occasionally he'd say something that reminded her of the way they'd met, and she'd laugh against her own better judgment, even while she quietly threatened him with bodily harm if he dared to tell anyone else what had happened Friday night.

There was more than flirtation, though. More than that bad-boy grin, or the knowing smirk. At one point, when she'd been busy helping Anna bring out side dishes and condiments, she realized Xander had gone back to the magnolia tree and finished what she'd started this afternoon. She'd found a half dozen magnolia blooms piled up on the table in front of her vacant chair. They were in full, creamy-colored bloom. Fragrant, soft, exquisite.

When she raised a curious brow, he shrugged. "I didn't want you to risk any more raging dragonfly attacks," he told her. "I might not be around to catch you next time."

The gesture made her melt a little, deep inside. "I'm not the type of woman who waits around for a man to catch me."

"That's okay, I won't make you wait."

They stared at one another for a long moment, then she lifted the blooms in her arms, bringing the entire bunch to her face and inhaling deeply. Rubbing the petals against her face, she smiled in contentment as the lovely fragrance filled her nose.

Looking over the armful of flowers, she saw Xander was still watching her closely. He lifted a hand and rubbed his jaw, his eyes narrowing as he studied her. She saw his throat move as he swallowed hard and realized he was affected by her sensual delight in the flowers—their scent, their beauty, their softness. After a moment's hesitation, she drew the bouquet close again, brushing the petals of one across her lips.

She heard his tiny, almost inaudible groan. He shifted a little closer and inhaled, as if wanting to share the moment, and the warmth of his tall, rock-hard body radiated toward her.

"I'd never even seen real magnolias before I moved to Georgia," he murmured, reaching up and scraping the tip of his index finger against one big blossom.

"They're my…"

"Favorite flower," he concluded. "I know."

Of course he did, she'd told him earlier. But she suspected that even if she hadn't, he'd have realized it. He was intuitive; he noticed things.

She suddenly had the strangest thought—did Dimitri know her favorite flower?

All the things Xander had said about how little Dimitri knew her had stuck in her brain, gnawing at her.

Did Dimitri know how badly she sometimes just needed to let her hair down and laugh? Did he realize how much of her real self she subdued every day in order to fit in to the world she wasn't even sure she liked? Did he know what she wanted, and how she wanted it…which sounded like an incredibly sexual question but could really be applied to every part of her life?

Did he even know her real name?

Honestly, in all the time they'd known each other, he'd never made the perceptive comments Xander had made to her today. And he'd never asked her what Mimi stood for.

That was the moment when she realized she might

have made a big mistake. Because, up until then, being around a sexy, flirtatious guy was just a little dangerous. Now she realized she was spending time with a very perceptive and very nice one, too. Nice. Sexy. Smart. Charming.

And, uh, *not* the guy she was dating. Not the one who had been handpicked by her father. Not the one who fit into her neatly ordered future. Not the one who was low-risk, who wouldn't hurt her.

Oh, she was in serious trouble here.

"You know," she said, suddenly lowering the flowers and turning away from Xander, "it's getting late and it's a work night. I think I'm going to head in."

"Thanks for your help, honey," said Anna. "Let's do this again next Saturday to welcome my daughter and grandson, okay?"

"*Our* daughter and grandson," Obi-Wan interjected.

Anna ignored him. "Helen and Tuck will be arriving from Atlanta late Saturday afternoon."

"I know you must be very happy about that," Mimi said.

"We are," said Obi-Wan. "Our daughter needs us. *Both* of us."

He and his wife exchanged a look, and Anna slowly nodded in agreement. Here, at least, they would always be united. Maybe having Helen and Tuck around would be good for them…if they had a joint cause, perhaps they wouldn't allow petty misunderstandings to keep them apart. Of course, even if Anna gave up her Shakespearean "boy-toy," something else would happen to set off Obi-Wan's jealous streak again in a few months. Still, a few months' peace would be good for everyone.

Saying good-night again, and ignoring Xander's curious—somewhat accusing—stare, she went inside.

While she hadn't been kidding about needing to head in because it was a work night, she had a problem. She wasn't tired. Not at all. She couldn't stop thinking about the day, the way Xander had plucked her out of the air like some kind of swashbuckling hero. That sounded familiar to her, for some reason—probably from some romantic movie she'd seen. Nor could she stop replaying their conversations, both personal and not, both serious and light.

After taking a long shower, she tried watching TV, then reading. She was alert for sounds in the hall, and knew exactly when the house party broke up. Which meant she also knew when Xander was back in his apartment, alone. Probably getting ready for bed. She hoped he had a better night's sleep than she was in store for, because she didn't think she'd manage to close her eyes for hours.

Then, suddenly, she remembered something. "The tea!"

There was more of Obi-Wan's wonderfully soothing tea in the small bag he'd given her Friday night. She couldn't remember exactly how it tasted, she just knew it had helped her fall asleep almost immediately. She'd slept like the dead, hadn't been conscious of a thing until the next morning and had awakened feeling refreshed and full of energy.

Heading into the kitchen, she brewed a cup. As she stirred it and carried it back to her room, the aroma tickled her nostrils and that familiar warmth hit her.

But it wasn't until she actually took her first sip that something else did.

Memories.

"That crazy dream," she mumbled, suddenly remembering the strange adventure with the dragon and the flying man. "Weird."

She didn't imagine the tea had caused the dream, but it had apparently knocked her out enough to make her forget all about it until just now. It was potent stuff.

So potent that she was asleep again within minutes of finishing the cup.

Asleep…and dreaming…

It was evening. Not yet dark—minutes before sunset, perhaps. The sky was a sherbet-swirl blend of pink, orange and purple. The day's last golden sunbeams pierced the clear sky, sending warmth cascading down on the earth, a shower of sun drops, a heavy rain of dazzling heat. Mimi felt it sizzling on her skin, warming every inch of her.

Something had beckoned her outside—a scent. A musky, masculine smell filled her nostrils and intoxicated her, sending pulsing need flowing through her veins. She needed to follow it, breathe it in, let it fill her completely. She was drawn to its source as if pulled irrevocably forward by invisible strings that had latched around her body.

She was walking in the woods, surrounded by ancient trees, loops of vines, the greens and browns of nature's forest palette. When she inhaled, the air tasted of pine, oaky bark and musky earth. And man. Oh, delightful, hot, spicy man.

Thick moss carpeted her toes. Despite the heat, and that perfect, cloudless sky, there was still a low mist hovering over the ground. She felt it swirling around her ankles, soft, warm, moist fingers of air caressing her skin, sliding up her calves, kissing her thighs.

She realized she was naked. But there was no embarrassment, no clasping of arms over bare breasts, or hand over the vulnerable thatch of curls concealing her sex. She was unashamed, untamed, free and natural. All that was elemental and earthy and right.

She was Eve.

And there, lying beside a bubbling brook, was her Adam.

Another man's name flashed in her mind, though it really had no meaning. She couldn't quite remember who that was, nor could she be sure the name belonged to the naked man lying before her, one arm flung out to his side, the other bent and draped over his face.

She breathed in, searching for the scent that had so attracted her, but must have been too far away, because she didn't catch it.

So she just looked. Stared. It was impossible not to.

He was beautiful. Tall, lean and strong, with muscles flexing beneath his warm skin. He was unaware of her, merely warming himself in the sun, his sex flaccid, his mood languid and relaxed. Like a big cat lazing on a sunny rock.

She knew she should leave him, walk away, not interrupt his idyll. But instead, her feet moved forward. As she drew closer, she noted the light swirl of hair on his chest, which rose and fell with his steady breaths.

The skin was glistening, a faint sheen of sweat visible on the rippling muscles of his stomach.

He shifted, arched up a little. Then he inhaled deeply, as if catching some scent in the air—as drawn to hers as she was to his. It must have been his, mustn't it? She edged closer, needing her senses filled with it again, but still didn't get what she sought.

He moved his arm away from his face and looked toward her, but the mist still obscured his face. When he murmured, "Come," she thought she recalled the voice.

Dimitri.

But who was Dimitri? She couldn't quite recall.

He waited, but she hesitated, the mist seeming to hold tight to her ankles. This was what she wanted, wasn't it? The moment she'd planned for, waited for? So why did she remain in the shadows, her feet heavy, her body tense?

She was quiet, waiting, thinking. And then, suddenly, she could smell it again. Her body reacted to the heat of man smell, the richness of sex and desire and passion. It called to her, aroused her, filled her with need and hunger, as if she were an animal reacting to the pheromones of her mate.

Her mind leaped forward and her feet wanted to follow, but she had the strangest feeling that something was behind her. A crush of leaf and twig hinted that someone was even closer to her than she was to the nude man lying on the ground. There was a faint stirring in the air, then the oddest sensation of warmth, like a slowly released breath, brushed her nape.

Her nerve endings awakened, her heart thumping

in her chest. Her blood heated and thickened in her veins as she waited.

Then it happened. Someone touched her—a finger of sensation gliding down her spine, from her neck, all the way to the cleft of her bottom, brushing lightly over every vertebrae, bringing every nerve ending roaring to life. She didn't flinch, was not startled. Instead, she was tingling, aware and anxious, waiting for the next touch, the next breath, a whisper.

But that whisper came from in front of her, not behind.

"Come here."

Dimitri was waiting. He'd been waiting, patiently, quietly. The right man. The one she was supposed to be with.

Mimi felt torn, confused. He was in front of her, but also behind her? It seemed anything was possible in this magical wood. So finally her feet started to move.

She walked slowly, staring straight ahead, yet ever so aware that she might be leaving something wonderful behind her, unexplored.

She reached him, and he lifted a hand in welcome. Staring down at his beautiful body, she thought that he must be an artist's model come to life. He was perfectly proportioned, not too big, not too small. Just the right amount of sparse hair on his chest, exactly the perfect dimension of hip to chest.

"I've been waiting," he said. "I want to shower you with red roses and diamonds."

"Just bring me to life," she replied, not wanting any of those things.

She lifted one leg over him, straddling him, then low-

ered herself onto his body. His soft cock was nestled in her curls, its moist tip pressing gently against her clit, like a warm tongue.

"Mmm," she groaned.

He reached up, tangled his hands in her hair and drew her down for a kiss. Their mouths met, lips parting, tongues licking slowly. It was warm and easy. Not like flying, more like falling.

It was good. But not good enough.

She grabbed his shoulders, digging her fingers into his muscles, trying to tell him she wanted more. Needed more. He didn't seem to understand, continuing the lazy, sensual assault that teased but didn't satisfy, flicking a spark but never igniting.

She whimpered, pressing harder against him, noting that the long ridge of masculine flesh between her thighs, pressed into the lips of her sex, remained half-flaccid. Frustration washed over her and she began to shake. She ended the kiss, tempted to throw herself off him.

That tingling sensation began again. The hairs at her nape stood up and her body arched instinctively, her bottom curving back and up. Her eyes dropped closed and she waited, tuning in to her other senses.

And there it was—oh, that smell. The musky, masculine scent that had drawn her into the forest to begin with flooded the air, and with it came pure heat.

She froze, still straddling Dimitri, her thighs clenched around his naked hips. She turned her head, but before she could see the forest god of heat and musk and male, she felt his hot mouth on her neck. She cried out. Dropping her head to the side to give him access, she cooed as he sucked her skin, nipping at her. Not gently. But passion, not pain, was the driving factor.

"Mine. You're mine," he growled, emphasizing the claim by grabbing her hips with his big, calloused hands. He squeezed, tugging her up until she was kneeling directly in front of him. One big arm curled around her waist, his hand moving up to catch her naked breast. She shook, she shuddered, she cried.

His fingers stroked her aching nipple, tweaking, pinching lightly, and her hips jerked reflexively as she felt the touch down to her very core.

"Mine," he repeated, that mouth hot against her neck. "I'm the one you want."

She arched back against him, groaning, and was rewarded with the feel of his massive form pressed against her. He was naked, sweaty, his crisp body hair spiking her with sensation, from the chest that seemed twice as broad as her back, all the way down his stomach, to the wiry nest rubbing against her bottom. And from it sprang what felt like an utterly enormous, thick and fully erect cock.

"Yes," she cried, every sense roaring to life, every inch of her in tune to the sensations that battered her like the strong winds of a hurricane. Liquid want flooded her sex and she was dying to be filled by him. She desperately wanted to turn around, to see his face, to behold the incredibly sensual creature seducing her right out of the arms of another naked man.

"No, she's mine," that other man said. "I'm the one she's supposed to be with."

She looked down. The man with the mist-swathed face still lay below her. She could see the angry thrust of his sculpted jaw, the snarl on his lips. And she felt between her thighs that his penis, only half in the game before, had come roaring to awareness. He was long and rock-hard against her skin, just a few teasing inches away from her opening. As if the very thought of someone else wanting her—taking her—had pushed him over the edge.

He rose up on an elbow, reaching for her, his mouth moving to her other breast. When he covered it with his lips and gently suckled, she cried out. His mouth pleasured one side while the dark forest god's hand and fingers tweaked heaven on the other.

Mimi closed her eyes again, giving herself over to it, lost in her other senses. Her skin was on fire, her pleasure receptors attacked from every direction. Hands were on her hips, her breasts, her thighs, her butt. Hoarse, hungry groans warred with the sound of her own heartbeat. She tasted sex every time she opened her mouth to draw breath. She smelled the forest and the trees and the earth and sweat and cock and skin and breath and musk and cum and magnolias and moss and her head was ready to explode as she tried to take it all in.

The hand on her bottom moved down, dipping between her cheeks. She quivered at the wicked touch as he explored her. She arched her back, urging him onward. His fingertips slid into her slick lips, and she cried out, jerking into his hand. Those strong fingers found her clit, stroked it, circled it, played it like a tiny instrument until she was shaking. If not for his other arm around her, his other hand still cupping her breast, she might have fallen.

Right onto the other man, whose mouth had moved to explore her ever so much more intimately.

Oh, God.

He was edging lower, shifting his entire body through her parted legs so he could reach more of her vulnerable skin. She was now kneeling right above his face. His tongue teased her stomach, dipped into her belly button. Then he slid down even farther, his lips nuzzling her curls, until his tongue replaced the dark stranger's fingers, leaving those fingers free to move back to her opening. Thick heat as one entered her. Another joined it, slowly thrusting in and out.

She was crying by this point, tears of erotic pleasure flowing from her eyes. The first orgasm blasted through her, and she shook, falling forward, having to brace herself on her hands. She was on all fours, one lover below her, one behind her.

They moved as if choreographed. The man on the ground—she could no longer recall his name, the one she'd been using didn't seem to fit anymore—kissed his way back up until he was able to reach her breasts, catching one with his hand, the other with his mouth. She looked down at him, startled to realize she could see him better now. The mist had shifted, and she caught a glimpse of nearly jet-black hair, coarse and thick and a little long. That seemed strange to her, unexpected, as she thought his hair had been lighter, golden-brown, when she'd first stumbled over him in the tiny glen. His body seemed bigger somehow, more rugged and rough, the chest hair thicker, darker, his muscles far more bulky and commanding.

He had changed, become someone else. At some

point, he'd segued from someone she wasn't sure she wanted into someone she was aching for. But the mist shifted again, and she couldn't fathom who he was.

Mimi felt too good to care, too aroused to question. She was practically dying now, needing the scene to climax, even if her body already had, at least once. She need to be filled. By one of them. By both of them. Now.

She felt the other—the delicious-smelling stranger she had never even seen—move in tight behind her, his enormous cock nudging between the curves of her ass. She shimmied up and down, wetting him, inviting him, then held her breath, waiting for him to accept the invitation. The thick, huge tip of him nestled closer, teasingly traipsing across her rear opening, then nudging between the swollen lips of her sex.

She held her breath, anticipation flooding her, then finally felt him edge into her body. An inch—she whimpered. Another—she sighed. Another—she was groaning now.

Then his hands clutched her hips and he groaned himself, plunging deep and hard, as if unable to draw this out anymore.

This time, she screamed. He filled her up so deeply, so powerfully, she felt she might break apart. But it was good. So damn good, she honestly didn't think she'd ever experienced such heady pleasure.

Her other lover twined his hands in her hair and drew her down for a kiss. His mouth was no longer soft and tender; this kiss was hot, deep, hungry. It was like she was kissing another man, different from the one she'd kissed before.

His scent was also familiar now. So incredibly rich

and evocative. It was the scent she'd come to associate with the dark stranger riding her from behind.

He was both men. Taking her wildly, thrusting into her with hard, hungry strokes, and yet still below her, kissing her, stroking her breasts, making love to her mouth with his tongue. The same dark, dangerous, powerful stranger. It made no sense, yet she realized it was true. He surrounded her. He was on all sides, in all places, taking her to heights of pleasure she hadn't even realized were possible.

Then he took her one step higher, and she broke apart into a million satisfied pieces.

She fell, dropping onto him, curling her face into his neck. She was limp, boneless, able to do nothing but lie there and let the last waves of her powerful orgasm dissipate beneath the evening sun. He was still surrounding her, stroking her tenderly, kissing her hair, whispering in her ears, as, still bathed in the glow of ultimate delight, she fell asleep.

6

EVEN THOUGH HE was a lieutenant, as the new guy, Xander had had to pull some strings to get a weekend off for his move-in to his new apartment from the extended-stay hotel where he'd been living. So he didn't complain about the back-to-back shifts that hit him over the next week. Hell, he'd done crazy hours from the time he started volunteering at a firehouse as a teenager.

The guys in the squad had been friendly from the minute he walked through the door, even though some of them might very well resent him for coming in from out of state and walking into a supervisory position. So far, though, he'd had no real problems with anybody, and had, a couple of times, even gone out for an after-an-overnight-shift breakfast, or after-a-day-shift beer with some of his coworkers.

But by late Saturday afternoon, when he returned home after thirty-six hours straight in a firehouse with a bunch of dudes, he really just wanted to chill out and relax. Remembering the plans his landlady had mentioned last weekend, he figured the whole B.Y.O.M. cookout would be a great way to do it.

Especially because Mimi would almost certainly be there.

He'd seen her several times throughout the week, but for the most part, they'd nodded, said "Good morning," or "Good night," and gone their separate ways.

She was avoiding him. No doubt about it.

He couldn't say why, considering how intimate their conversations had been last weekend, but he knew it was true. She didn't meet his eye as readily, didn't smile as freely. Tension rolled off her and he'd swear the one time they physically brushed against one another while getting the mail, she'd actually flinched. It was as if sometime Sunday night, between the flirting and the flowers, she'd decided to put up a wall between them and stay on her side of it.

He couldn't deny, it bugged him. The only thing that bugged him more was that Dimitri had come by twice this week. Once to pick her up and take her to work because her car was in the shop. And once, it looked like, to take her to a fancy dinner.

Xander had bumped into them on their way out. Plastic Dude had been perfectly dressed, all suited up, right down to a flash of gold cuff links at his wrists. Mimi had looked beautiful, of course, but also pale. A little strained.

He would chalk it up to trouble in paradise, but he knew better. That relationship was going absolutely nowhere—anyone could see it, except, perhaps for Dimitri. But Mimi knew. Her eyes were open, she just wasn't ready to admit it yet.

Xander just wondered how long it was going to

take…and whether or not he'd have the patience to wait her out.

Then he thought about the way she'd kissed him, the way she'd felt in his arms, the taste of her mouth, the smell of her hair. And knew he'd wait as long as it took.

He was still smiling at that thought as he parked his car in the driveway late Saturday afternoon. Walking around it toward the house, he caught a glimpse of something colorful out of the corner of his eye, over near the edge of the woods. Curious, he glanced over, just in time to see a figure dressed in bright yellow disappear into the trees.

He'd recognize that red hair anywhere.

Why are you going into the woods? he wondered.

It was none of his business, and he didn't even think about following her. Mimi had avoided him all week. The next time the line in the sand got crossed, it would have to be because she'd decided to cross it.

Of course, all his determination and certainty about that flew right out the window when he heard a child's scream.

He froze in place. Then, not giving it another thought, spun on his heels and ran across the lawn. His feet pounded the ground, digging up clods of grass, and he didn't even hesitate as he plowed between thick trees and vines, merely shoving them out of the way with his extended hands.

The voice yelled again. "Watch out!"

"Mimi?"

"Catch him!"

He followed the sound and burst into a clearing. Standing at the base of a huge tree was a little boy, probably about six or seven, with a curly mop of light brown hair, a million freckles and anxious eyes. He was staring up at a massive live oak.

And in that live oak was Mimi.

"What the hell?" he said, moving closer. "What's going on?"

"She's saving Buster, my cat," the boy exclaimed. "He got up the tree and can't get down and he's gonna fall if she doesn't save him."

Mimi had climbed up several limbs and was now about twenty feet off the ground, and all he could think was, *And who's going to save her?*

"Damn it, Mimi, get down from there."

"Xander?" She peered down at him from above. "No worries—I'm not on a shaky ladder this time. And I checked for bees."

He rolled his eyes and gritted his teeth. "Would you please climb back down here?"

"But Buster's scared," the boy said. "We can't just leave him up there." He immediately made to climb the tree himself, but couldn't reach so much as the bottom limb.

"You stay put," Xander told him. He moved past the boy and swung himself up onto the nearest branch and began working his way up. "Mimi, I'm coming."

"Don't be silly, I'm fine," she insisted.

And she might have been. Only the stuck, loudly meowing Buster had other ideas. He chose that moment to leap from branch to branch, catching Mimi's arm with a sharp claw, sending her sliding downward.

"Ow!" she cried, continuing to scrape her way down, unable to grab hold of another branch. She wrapped her arms around the trunk and slid, her legs swinging as she tried to find support.

Fortunately, Xander was there to give it to her. His heart racing, he dove against the trunk directly below her, giving her his body to land on. Her feet came to rest on his shoulders. With an *oomph,* he grabbed her ankles, steadying her. From below they probably looked like a circus act. Two clowns in a tree.

"I've got you."

"Who's got you?"

"Good question. Hold still."

She did. Unfortunately, the cat didn't. It used Mimi as a stepladder, hopping from her arm to her shoulder—tangling a paw in her hair and eliciting a squeal of pain—then skidding down her back and onto Xander's head.

"Don't move, cat," he told the hissing animal, reaching to try to grab it with one hand, while holding Mimi's ankle with the other.

The feline ignored him, leaping nimbly to the lowest branch, then right down into the extended arms of the boy waiting on the ground below. Safe, and completely oblivious to the mischief he'd caused.

"Buster," the boy said, "you're in big trouble. Mom said we weren't supposed to leave the yard." He spared a glance up. "Thanks, lady, mister. I should get back now."

Then, as unconcerned as all kids were once their dramas are over, he skipped out of the clearing, not waiting to see if Mimi was going to make it down. Or if Xander was going to spank her butt for climbing up so high—again—without anyone around to help her. He was seriously considering it.

"I'm going to step out from under you and hold your legs to help guide you down," he said.

"Are you sure?"

"Got any better ideas?"

She looked down at him, blowing a long strand of hair out of her face, then shook her head.

"What is it with you, me and this position?" he muttered as he looked up at what was becoming his very favorite view.

She grunted, glared, then began to move. Slowly. Carefully.

Gripping her calves, he helped her lower one, and then the other, off his shoulder. His arms flexed, his muscles tightening as he supported her entire body. Little by little, he let her long limbs slide through his hands. Down, down, down she came, until she was standing on the same huge limb, her back to him, still hugging the trunk.

He literally breathed a sigh of relief. Sliding one arm around her waist, he tugged her back against him, holding her close. He couldn't stop himself from burying his face in her hair, his mouth against her neck, so close he could feel her raging pulse fluttering against his lips.

"You're okay," he whispered, reassuring them both.

"Thanks to you," she replied. She dropped her head back until it rested on his chest, and leaned a little so he had better access to her neck.

He took advantage, kissing her pulse point, then the spot directly behind her ear. She was pressed tightly against him, the pose provocative, her posture willing and pliant. His thoughts were racing crazily, from what might have been had she fallen to what might be now that she was pressing back against him like she wanted to make their clothes disappear.

"Are you sure you're all right?" he asked, carefully turning her around to face him.

"I'm sure." She smiled up at him, then reached up and swiped her thick hair off her face. Her cheek was smudged with dirt and a tiny bit of blood where either the cat's claws or the tree's bark had nicked her. A few leaves were tangled in her curls, and she had a sappy pine needle stuck to her chin.

And she looked beautiful. So incredibly beautiful.

He was well over his desire to spank her, and went right for the I'm-so-relieved-you're-okay reaction. He drew her into his arms and hauled her against him, not even caring that they were still a good six or seven feet above solid ground.

She threw her arms around his neck, holding on, and neither of them hesitated before diving together in a hot, hungry kiss. Their tongues met and mated, swirling and exploring. After not having tasted her for a week, he felt like he was ending a hunger strike. She provided all the nourishment he needed, her sweet taste heightened by her sultry woman's smell.

She shimmied even closer, and he braced a hand behind her, on the tree trunk, to keep them stable as the kiss continued. Everything else disappeared—time, place, the kid, the cat, the job, the other guy. All of it. At least for a little while.

Finally, though, when his body was throbbing with need to do a lot more than kiss, he slowed things down.

Because as much as he wanted to continue, there was, of course, the small problem that they were still standing in a tree.

When they finally drew apart to heave in a few breaths, he said, "I thought you weren't the type to wait around for a man to catch you."

"Well, just like you promised—you didn't make me wait."

They both smiled. Then, by unspoken agreement, began to climb down out of the tree. Xander helped her with the final drop, noticing the way she flinched when his hands encircled her waist. "Are you hurt?"

They both glanced down. During her descent, her bright yellow top had been pulled free of the waistband of her white capris. Now, both shirt and pants were ripped and smeared with stains.

Tugging the shirt up a little, she revealed several flecks of blood on her stomach from where she'd brushed against the rough bark. "Ow," she mumbled.

"Let me see," he said, dropping to one knee in front of her for a closer look. He pushed her shirt up higher. Her creamy skin was reddened and scraped in several places, but there were no deep cuts. Still, it had to sting. "You're going to need to clean these up and put some antiseptic on them," he said. He lifted a hand and brushed his fingertip right beside the worst scrape. "Especially this one."

She made a tiny sound of assent. He looked up and saw Mimi had closed her eyes and dropped her head back a little.

She did not look like a woman in pain.

She looked like a woman who'd just been thoroughly

kissed, whose partner in that kissing was now kneeling at her feet, inches away from her delectable body.

Xander could have stood back up, brought her back to the house to tend her cuts. But something compelled him to lean close…then closer. Until his mouth hovered an inch over one of the scrapes. He eliminated that inch, pressing a soft, gentle kiss on the sore. *Kissing it better.*

She didn't resist, didn't pull away. Instead, she slid her hands into his hair, twining strands around her fingers.

Xander moved to another spot, sliding his lips ever so lightly across her stomach, his jaw brushing against the fabric of her cropped pants. They were low-waisted enough to reveal her belly button and he moved there, swirling his tongue over that tiny indentation.

"Xander," she groaned.

He ignored her, moving again, breathing through the thin cotton. He could smell her now, smell that secret, feminine scent that called to each masculine cell in his body and made it spark. She was aroused. Warm and wet beneath her clothes. And while he was dying to feel her, taste her more fully, right now he was content to merely breathe in her essence.

She dropped her hands to his shoulders. He moved his to encircle her hips, stroking that perfectly curved feminine bottom, urging her closer. He knew he should stop, knew it was broad daylight. But they were surrounded by trees, wrapped in the secretive embrace of the woods. He couldn't stop. He just couldn't. She'd been nearly naked when he'd fallen at her feet that first night. And ever since, he'd dreamed about exploring that beautiful, secret place he'd been privileged enough to see.

He opened his mouth, tasting her through the fabric, letting her feel the heat of his breath. Letting her pull away if she felt she had to.

She sighed and arched closer. Which was all the answer he needed to the question he hadn't even asked.

He slid his fingertips into her waistband, unbuttoned it and gently tugged her pants down. Sighing again, she leaned back against the tree, as if her legs could no longer bear her full weight.

At some point, he'd love to lay her down in a bed and pleasure her until she couldn't remember her own name. But right now, being below her, looking up at her, seemed like the perfect way to do what he'd been wanting to do for days.

Xander kissed each spot of skin as it was revealed, loving the flavors of her. She quivered as first his breath, then his lips, then his tongue touched the vulnerable indentation just above her panties. When he moved them down so he could brush his lips against her soft curls, she groaned out loud.

"Oh, God."

"I've wanted to taste you since the night we met," he admitted. "Don't stop me."

She didn't stop him.

One flick and he'd pushed the pants and her panties down all the way to the ground, revealing that beautiful thatch of amber curls between her thighs. It invited him, tempted him beyond belief, and he didn't have the patience to tease her anymore. He slid his tongue between the plump lips of her sex, finding her hard little clit immediately.

She let out a cry, her hands tightening on his shoulders. Xander lifted his hands to her bottom to hold her tight, squeezing her, tilting her closer so he could offer her even more pleasure.

She took it, welcoming him with an arch of her hips, and he continued to stroke her sensitive nub with his tongue. He sucked it, nibbled it, changed the pressure, knowing by her cries what she liked the best. When she began to pant, then to shake, he slowed things down a bit. Yes, he was tormenting her—but the payoff would be even better if he made her wait.

"Xander," she begged when he moved his mouth away.

"I need to taste all of you," he muttered as he licked his way down the sweet, slick folds of her sex.

He pushed her back harder against the tree, wanting access to all of her now. Pushing her pants off one foot, he lifted it, draping her leg over his shoulder, parting her fully to the bright daylight and his hungry gaze. When he saw all her feminine glory, his mouth watered. He wanted to drink from her, to savor her and swallow her down.

He plunged deep, making love to her with slow, steady strokes of his tongue. She shuddered, whispering his name, begging for more, begging him to stop, ordering him not to.

All his senses were overwhelmed with Mimi—the brush of her soft thigh against his cheek, the beauty of the secret, feminine flesh he couldn't stop exploring, the taste of her on his tongue, her joyful cries in his ears.

He wanted to really make love to her. He was desperate to free his throbbing, aching cock from the confinement of his jeans and plunge up into the warm, welcoming heat that wrapped around his tongue. Knowing he couldn't, he made a mental note to always carry a condom from this point on.

"Please, please…"

He knew what she needed, knew she craved release with desperation that bordered on insanity. So he moved his mouth back up to that pretty little clit. He licked it, toyed with it, timing his strokes to the sound and volume of her cries.

It didn't take long. With one more deep, pleasure-filled groan, she jerked hard and dug her nails into his shoulders.

"Yes, oh, yes," she said, shaking against him for several long moments. When at last the shudders began to subside, she was apparently left weak-kneed. She sank down to the ground in front of him, her arms draped across his shoulders. Xander tugged her tightly to him and she collapsed against his chest, her face buried in the crook of his neck. She was panting, gasping for air, her whole body quivering, still reacting to every sensation, fully affected by what they'd just done.

Xander was panting and shaking, too. But at this point, it was sheer need making him quake. He needed to be in her and not being able to was just about killing him.

"Mimi!" a voice called. "Are you back there?"

Hearing the intrusion, Mimi flew back so fast she landed on her bare butt on the ground. Her eyes wide with panic, she scrambled to pull her clothes back into place.

"Calm down, I'll stall," he said, leaping to his feet, then pulling her to hers. He'd recognized their landlady's voice. "We're on our way, Anna. Be right there!" he called.

"Oh, my God, what were we thinking?" Mimi whispered, still frantically trying to get her clothes into place.

"The same thing we've both been thinking for seven days and twenty or so hours." Xander pushed her hands out of the way, twisting her capris into the right position, then tucked her shirt in. "It's okay. Breathe."

"That's easy for you to say, you didn't just..."

"Uh, I think I had something to do with it."

She looked up at him, those violet eyes wide and luminous. Her lips quivered. "Yes. You did. Thanks."

"Always a pleasure," he said with a wag of his eyebrows.

She snagged her bottom lip between her teeth, but was unsuccessful at containing a giggle. There was no regret, no anger, no guilt. She looked...happy. Joyful. As if being intimate with him, here, in the woods, was the most natural, wonderful thing in the world.

"Ready?" he asked, reaching for her hand.

"Yes," she said, falling into step beside him. Then, with a sheepish shrug, she added, "You, uh, might want to wipe your face."

He didn't. He really didn't. He wanted to smell her and taste her for the rest of the night. But considering they could see their landlady standing at the edge of the lawn, he figured he ought to do what he could to hide what they'd been up to.

He pulled his shirt up, wiping off the remnants of Mimi's arousal from his lips and cheeks, knowing there was no way to wipe off his self-satisfied smile. Nor could anything eliminate the aura of satisfaction wafting off the thoroughly pleasured woman at his side.

"There you are!" Anna exclaimed as she caught sight of them. "You have surprise guests, Mimi. Dimitri is here, and he has someone else with him."

She stumbled. If he hadn't had her hand clasped in his, she might have fallen. A lump rising in his throat, he cast her a quick, reassuring look, and realized he had been wrong. There was something that could eliminate that aura of pleasure wafting off her: houseguests.

Talk about your bad timing.

Seeing Anna's curious look, Xander glanced down at their clasped hands. Mimi did, too, and immediately let go, her hand dropping to her side.

Anna pretended she hadn't noticed. "Thank you for rescuing Tuck's cat."

Tuck. The grandson, if he remembered correctly. He and his mother were moving in today. Obviously Buster the feline was exploring his new home.

"Not a problem," Mimi said, her voice low, toneless.

Hearing that lifelessness, Xander wanted to break something. Mimi had been an earthy angel in his arms a few minutes ago. Now she was being thrust right back into real life with the guy she'd been dating.

Only, no. No way. She wasn't going to be able to slip back into that role, to go back to being another man's sort-of girlfriend, not after what they'd just shared in the woods. "Mimi," he said, "we should..."

"We'll talk later, okay?" she insisted.

She picked up her pace, almost jogging to get ahead of him, heading for two men who stood on the back porch. Whether she was racing to her visitors or away from a conversation about them—what had happened, what it meant—he couldn't say.

"Uh, you might want to tuck in your shirt," Anna said, sounding only slightly amused.

"Thanks," he said, doing as she'd suggested.

"And I wouldn't suggest getting close enough to shake hands." She had the courtesy not to say *because you reek of illicit sex,* but it was understood.

As they continued to approach the patio where Mimi was talking with Dimitri and an older man who had to be her father, Anna spoke. "Don't give up on her, okay?"

Give up? Those words weren't even in his vocabulary. Especially not when they concerned Mimi. "Not gonna happen."

As they drew closer, he had no problem recognizing the human Ken doll, who, even when dressed in casual clothes, wore that aura of money that always clung to guys like him.

The other man was older, probably in his mid-fifties, with gray hair and a tan. Wearing white pants and a collared shirt with a polo player on the breast, he appeared ready to sip a martini at the ninth hole. The guy looked like he'd stepped off the pages of that old Richie Rich comic, as the character's dad.

"Dad, I still can't believe you decided to just stop by," Mimi said, sounding shocked.

Xander sighed, not truly surprised Mr. Rich had turned out to be her father.

"Dimitri and I were heading back from Arbor Ridge and realized how close we were, so we decided to drop in to visit."

Judging by their clothes and sun-reddened faces, Xander assumed Arbor Ridge was a golf course. How… chummy.

He wondered how Mimi felt about it. Her hands were clenched at her sides, her smile tight, and she was not meeting his eye. Was she worried Dimitri had seen the leaves in her hair, noted the redness of her lips, known she was in the woods with Xander and formed his own conclusions? He'd be an idiot not to.

Part of him thought that might not be a bad idea. Another part—the part that realized this was the father of the woman he was becoming seriously addicted to—knew he had to make a getaway. Talk about one hell of a bad first impression. *Hello, sir. Why, yes, that is your daughter's arousal I'm wearing like an expensive cologne.*

Not cool.

He pivoted on his feet, prepared to walk away without another word. But Mimi's father spotted him and raised his voice to say, "Well, Mimi, are you going to introduce us?"

Xander kept walking a few paces, then glanced back, as if just realizing the older man had been talking about him. He smiled, nodding hello to Dimitri, noticing the way Mimi kept looking back and forth between all three of them, her frown deepening. Tension washed over her, as visible as if she'd been doused with a bucket of paint.

His heart twisted as he realized just how frazzled she was. The incredibly hot-and-sexy, joking, flashing, vase-threatening, vibrant woman appeared racked with uncertainty.

One way to help ease it.

"Sorry I can't stay for introductions," he called. "I have to head back to the station unexpectedly." *To shower.* "Anna, tell that grandson of yours to take care of his mischievous cat." Then, with a friendly smile at Mimi, he added, "And don't go climbing any more trees without backup, okay?"

He could almost see her exhale a sigh of relief, and she offered him a tremulous smile of thanks. "Definitely not."

Nodding pleasantly, he said, "Bye," then turned and left.

As he got into his car and drove back to the station, he told himself he was glad for the interruption. It wasn't as if he wouldn't have loved some more afternoon delight with Mimi, but the situation wasn't exactly ideal. Nor was the location.

The next time he touched her, it would be in a bed, or some other comfortable flat surface. And that couldn't come soon enough for him.

He didn't doubt that it would happen. It didn't matter what he'd told himself about whether she was right for him, or he for her, or that they hid the truth behind small talk and ladder adventures or cat rescues. It was there: attraction. Interest. Heat. It was seething. Growing.

It had caught fire today and burned brightly, if too briefly. Soon enough they'd start an inferno that wouldn't be doused until they'd done everything two consenting adults could do together. It was as given as the fact that the sun would rise and set tomorrow.

Sunrise. Sunset. And Mimi Burdette in his bed. They were the three most inevitable things in his life right now.

He was very curious to find out which would come first.

Deep down, he was betting on Mimi.

7

MIMI LOVED HER FAMILY—her parents, her aunts, uncles and cousins. But she also loved her privacy and her independence. That was one reason she'd insisted on moving into a small apartment and not into a large house of her own—she didn't *want* to have a place big enough for guests. She liked having a small sliver of life that didn't include anyone from her regular world. She liked stepping away from the Burdettes, away from the money, out from under the weight of social expectation. When she was here, with Anna and Obi-Wan and the others, she felt like she could be herself.

So while she was not churlish enough to be upset that her father had thought to stop by to say hello, she couldn't say she was thrilled about it, either. Especially because the timing had been beyond bad.

She wasn't sure whether to curse the interruption, or wish it had come ten minutes sooner.

Or ten minutes later.

Lots of things could have happened in ten minutes.

Despite having impromptu guests who showed no signs of wanting to leave, now that they'd settled in with some of Anna's famous sweet tea, she couldn't stop thinking about the crazy, shocking interlude she'd shared with Xander in the woods.

It wasn't just physical pleasure that caused her to dwell on every moment they'd spent together. The truth was, whenever she thought of the encounters she'd had with Xander so far, a smile came to her face and her heart started thudding in her chest like it had never thudded over Dimitri. That thudding was there whether she thought about him catching her as she fell off the ladder, or sharing a beer on a hot summer day.

Or kneeling at her feet, licking her into a serious case of temporary insanity.

"I hope you don't mind that I brought your dad here," Dimitri said, his voice low. "I did try to call to warn you. Guess you were already…outside."

She smiled in appreciation. Dimitri was a true Southern gentleman and he liked the niceties. Stopping by without an invitation was probably anathema to him.

So was asking why she'd been emerging from the woods, hand-in-hand with her new neighbor, when he'd arrived.

He'd seen them. Of that she had no doubt.

"It's okay. At least he has Anna and Obi-Wan on the same side for a change," she said, wishing her heart were as light as her faked tone.

They were sitting at the outside table, and her father, a prince of Wall Street, had engaged in a spirited political discussion with Mimi's landlords. That could only end badly; talk about the 1 percent versus the 99 percent.

Fortunately, her dad wasn't too much of a snob—he

was just pushy. Then again, he hadn't come up against a force as implacable and stubborn as the flower-power duo of Athens, Georgia, who, for once, weren't sniping at each other and were instead standing their tree-hugging ground.

She half wished Xander would come back, because she sensed he could cut through the B.S. and rhetoric and have everyone laughing over a beer in a very short time. He had already proved how good he was at putting people at ease last weekend.

Then again, he wouldn't be dealing with just Anna, Obi-Wan and the house's other residents this time. Dimitri already had a chip on his shoulder about him, and her father would if he so much as suspected Mimi's attention had drifted away from Dimitri.

God, what a mess.

Though she stayed out of the debate, disagreeing with her dad on a lot of points but not really caring enough to argue them, she noted that Dimitri did not. He quietly interjected support of her father where he could. Whether because he felt the same way, or just wanted to stick by the boss, she didn't know. She'd never pegged him for a suck-up; he was just a lot like the rest of her family in attitude and demeanor.

Why wasn't she?

She didn't know. Oh, sure, she had a few expensive tastes she occasionally indulged, like for good shoes. But for the most part, she far preferred drinking a beer and picnicking with her neighbors to attending some fancy party or country club formal. And she knew she'd had a much better time climbing or falling out of trees with Xander this week than she'd had when she'd gone out to dinner at an exclusive restaurant with Dimitri.

Maybe because drinking beer and climbing or falling out of trees had felt like the Mimi she was supposed to be. And being with Dimitri had felt like the Mimi everyone else expected her to be.

"Look who's finally back," Anna said, leaping up from her seat and hurrying over to the gate.

Mimi followed her gaze and saw the back gate opening and a very attractive, thirtyish woman enter the yard. The woman had short, curly brown hair and a broad smile that looked like Anna's, and was accompanied by a familiar little boy who owned an adventure-loving cat.

She'd met Tuck earlier, when he'd come looking for help to find Buster, but hadn't yet been introduced to his mom, Anna's daughter, Helen. They'd apparently been moving into 2B much of the day, but had gone out to pick up a few groceries and supplies after the great cat caper in the woods.

"Good God," she heard Dimitri mutter. He sounded stunned. "Helen?" His eyes were huge and something that looked like genuine pleasure crossed them for the briefest second.

Surprised, Mimi asked, "You know her?"

That was a coincidence, especially since Anna had told Mimi her daughter and grandson were moving from out of town and hadn't lived in Athens for years.

He didn't have to answer. The look of pleasure quickly disappeared, replaced by one of guilty shock. Not only did he know her, but he also wasn't exactly thrilled to see her, though whether that was dislike or embarrassment making his jaw clench, Mimi couldn't say. That first, honest, unguarded expression on his face sure hadn't looked like dislike.

Mimi rose from her chair as Anna led her daughter over and made introductions. Shaking Helen's hand, she in turn went on to introduce her father. But as she gestured toward Dimitri, she fell silent, wanting to see how the pretty woman reacted.

Strongly. The moment she saw him, her smile faded and her lips parted in a small gasp. "Dimitri?"

His smile forced, he said, "Good to see you again."

She froze, her stare moving over him from head to toe, as if she needed to double-check to make sure she could trust her eyes. Meanwhile everyone else stopped talking, stumbling into the awkward silence that had descended between two people who had some past connection nobody else knew anything about. If it wasn't a romantic one, Mimi would eat her one-and-only Coach bag.

She evaluated how she felt about it, waiting for some spark of jealousy or avid curiosity. Something that would indicate that, at least somewhere deep inside, a part of her felt some kind of claim on Dimitri. That was probably a little selfish, since she'd already acknowledged, at least to herself, that her thoughts, mind and body were totally engaged elsewhere. Still, she couldn't help wondering, since she had been dating the man, if her subconscious thought he was hers.

As it turned out, all she felt was curious.

And that was probably enough to answer the questions that had been plaguing her even before she'd met her hot new neighbor and started wondering what might have happened had he tripped six inches closer to her and landed a little bit higher.

Now she knew. Oh, Lordy, did she ever.

Nice to meet you, mouth, come and visit anytime.

"So, how do you two know each other?" Obi-Wan finally asked, his eyes slightly narrowed.

"We met in Atlanta last fall," Dimitri said. "Before I moved here."

"I didn't even know you left the city," Helen said, her voice soft, a hint of hurt in her eyes.

Meaning the relationship had meant more to her than to him.

"New job," he told her.

Beside him, Mimi's father finally caught the undercurrents and frowned. Mimi might not worry about a very attractive ex-girlfriend showing up to throw a wrench into the works, considering she was already trying to figure out how to let Dimitri know she didn't want to date him anymore, but her dad did. He'd cast Dimitri in the role of son-in-law, and had been waiting for Mimi to get with the program. Somebody else mucking things up was not part of his plan.

"Dimitri, if you're ready, we should be going." He pressed a kiss on Mimi's cheek. "Your mother's expecting me home."

"Give her my love and tell her we're on for lunch Wednesday." She and her mom had a standing weekly lunch date—it was always one of the highlights of her work week. Her mom couldn't be more different than her father when it came to the business, and Mimi always really enjoyed the social hour filled with talk about music, clothes and movies. Not bulk prices on toilet paper and close-out brands of vegetables. "Thanks for stopping by. It was nice."

Surprisingly, she meant it. She might have meant it more if he'd been alone, *really* just stopping by for a father-daughter visit. But he'd dragged Dimitri along. She wondered if Dimitri had said something over golf to make her father worry that his matchmaking plan was going awry.

"Uh, there's something I need to get from Mimi's place," Dimitri said, casting her an urgent glance. He obviously wanted a minute alone with her, probably to offer an explanation.

Though he didn't owe her one, she said, "Sure, come on in." Then, turning to her new neighbor, she smiled and added, "Helen, it's so nice to meet you. I've been looking forward to your arrival—it'll be great to have a kid around."

Right now, that kid was hanging upside down from the fence and he offered her a wave and a big grin. Next time his cat ran away, maybe the little monkey should climb the tree himself.

"You, too," Helen said. She cleared her throat and touched Dimitri's arm. "It was nice running into you."

"Yes. Good luck with your move," he said, shifting awkwardly from foot to foot. His hands were shoved in his pants pockets and he looked decidedly less sure of himself than usual.

Her father thanked Anna and Obi-Wan for the tea and the conversation, then left, saying he'd wait in the car. Leading the way, Mimi took Dimitri into her apartment. She had no sooner shut the door behind them when he launched into his story.

"I had no idea Helen was related to your landlords. We dated months ago. It was nothing."

She raised a brow. "I don't think she thought so."

"Mimi, I swear to you, we went out for a few weeks, max. She was in the middle of her divorce, nowhere near ready to be seeing anyone, and was an emotional mess. So I broke it off."

Dimitri wasn't the type who liked emotional scenes, she knew that much, so she could see why he wouldn't stick around for too much of somebody else's drama. Still, he wasn't an unkind person, and she couldn't see him intentionally kicking someone when they were down.

As if seeing her skepticism, he clarified, "Those were her words, by the way. Not mine. She's the one who said she was an emotional wreck, still half in love with her husband. So I bowed out."

That made more sense. Doing the right thing, "bowing out" sounded very Dimitri-like. She only wondered if that was why he'd had that look of happiness-mixed-with-pain on his face when he'd first seen Helen. Whatever the case, judging by the reactions of both of them, she would suspect things were a lot more complicated between Dimitri and Helen than he'd let on. But she didn't press him on it.

"Look, it's fine, really." Glancing out the window to where her father sat in Dimitri's car, probably already tapping his fingers in impatience, she added, "You don't owe me any explanations, Dimitri, it's none of my business how you feel about her. I mean, we're not..."

"Not what?"

Not in love, that was for sure. Not in a relationship.

Not heading for marriage and happily-ever-after... How could they be if she couldn't stop thinking about—*craving*—another man?

"We're not serious," she told him, starting there. "We've gone out a couple of times, that's all."

He hesitated, opening his mouth to say something, then closing it again. She waited for him to argue, waited for him to ask if she wanted to be, even waited for him to express some relief, since, somewhere deep down, he had to feel the same lack of chemistry she did.

Instead, he just said, "I should probably go or your father will start beeping the horn. Can we talk about this later?"

Hmm. Not exactly the acknowledgment she'd been going for. But it wasn't an argument, either. As usual, she had no idea what he was thinking. Damn, this strong-and-silent thing was getting on her nerves. She didn't know why she'd ever found it attractive in the first place.

Maybe because, until she'd met Xander, she hadn't really understood the appeal of a man who said exactly what he thought, and damn the consequences.

"Dimitri, I..."

The horn beeped. Good grief.

He actually rolled his eyes, which was about as close to annoyed as she'd ever seen him get with her father.

This was a conversation they needed to have. But knowing they couldn't get into anything serious with a honk underscoring every other sentence, she resigned herself to having to have it later. So when he murmured goodbye and brushed a kiss on her cheek, she smiled and let him go.

Once he was gone, she considered going back outside for the cookout, but Anna hadn't mentioned it since last weekend, and she didn't want to intrude on the family reunion. Nor did she want to do anything to make Helen unhappy on her first night back. If the woman was upset, thinking Dimitri had moved on and was dating Mimi, she might not appreciate the reminder.

In the end, she ended up eating a frozen dinner and watching a scary movie on TV. Which was probably a bad idea, because when it came time to go to bed, the Salisbury steak was sitting in her stomach like a cement block, and she was looking for shadows around every corner, certain every gleam of light was the reflection off a shiny knife.

She had just gotten changed into a lightweight summer nightgown when the thought of shiny knives made something else pop into her mind. "Damn. The scissors!"

This afternoon, when Tuck had come running, begging for help finding his erstwhile cat, Mimi had been in the backyard, carefully cutting some newly bloomed magnolias—from a *low-hanging* branch. She'd been using a pair of long, sharp shears, and, when she'd raced off into the woods after the boy, had left them lying at the base of the tree. When she'd come back to the house, she'd been so flustered by what had happened in the woods and by the arrival of her father and Dimitri, she'd completely forgotten to retrieve them.

They were large for scissors, but might not be easily visible to someone who wasn't on the lookout for them. In fact, they could lying there just waiting to be stumbled across by a rambunctious little boy. If Tuck went running around in the yard in the morning, wanting to explore his new home, he could either fall over them, or find them and decide to play with them. Either way, bad news.

She couldn't risk it. So, grabbing her robe and dragging it on over her baby-doll nightie, she slipped into her closet and felt her way along the back wall to the secret door. Thinking of the way Xander had come through here one week ago, she had to smile. And to wonder what kind of clothes were in the man's wardrobe if he had mistaken her silky blouses and dresses for anything he might have hanging in his own.

Outside, all was quiet. It was after midnight and everyone had likely gone inside hours ago. They'd turned off the backyard lights, which couldn't be accessed from her closet. While the starry, moonlit sky was bright enough, here inside the screen porch it was inky and black.

Twisted shadows, shapes and sounds from the movie crawled into her consciousness, making her tread carefully, wishing she'd thought to bring a flashlight. Not that she expected to stumble over an ax-wielding maniac on the patio, but hey, better safe than sorry.

Her hands out in front of her, she felt her way through the dark porch, trying to remember exactly where the outdoor furniture stood. She remembered too late that everything had been repositioned for the party last weekend and several extra chairs had been set up in here. She found one with her shin, banging into the edge of what felt like wrought iron.

"Ow," she said with a grunt, immediately bending down to cover the aching spot with her hand.

Which made her bump her shoulder into a portable bar Obi-Wan had bought and had decided to leave up for the summer.

Which made her spin out of the way and slam her hip into the back of a chaise lounge.

Over which she stumbled, landing right on top of it.

Well, to be more accurate, she landed right on top of the person who was reclining on it. Who, fortunately, wasn't wielding a knife. Just a wide, white smile, which he flashed at her in the darkness.

"Well, I was right, Mimi," a throaty, sexy voice rumbled. "You beat the sunrise."

XANDER DIDN'T QUESTION what had brought Mimi out onto the patio this late, dressed in what felt like that same silky, sexy-as-sin robe she'd been wearing the night they'd met. Like just about everything in his life, he simply went with it.

He certainly hadn't come out here hoping she might show up. He'd just been antsy, his internal clock off from a few overnight shifts this week. To make things worse, the cat-chasing rugrat who had moved in upstairs had apparently decided to see if he could bring down the 150-year-old house with his two stomping feet. So it seemed like a good idea to try sitting outside for a while, waiting the sleepless kid out.

Now, though, he was beginning to think he ought to buy the kid a bike or a video game tomorrow. Because he had definitely caused Xander to be in the right place at the right time. Twice.

"Xander? What are you doing out here?" yelped the

luscious armful of silky, satiny woman who'd landed in his arms like a gift from his fairy godmother.

"I could ask you the same question."

"I forgot something and was coming out to find it."

She was definitely on the verge of finding something. And the longer she remained sprawled on top of his nearly naked body—since he was wearing nothing but a pair of gym shorts—the closer she was to getting it.

"I couldn't sleep. Thought I'd get some fresh air," he admitted.

She'd landed on her side, and was draped across the entire length of him. She fit there perfectly, the top of her head brushing his cheek, the side of her breast pressed into his chest, her lush hip curving into his stomach.

Their bare legs were entwined, and he noted the way she moved hers up and down a little, as if by instinct, subconsciously wanting that frisson of excitement that came when soft, feminine skin rubbed firm masculine muscle.

He also noted that she wasn't trying to work her way off him, wasn't launching right up, wasn't rattling off excuses or apologies or trying to pretend he hadn't been on his knees licking her into a shattering orgasm a few hours ago. In fact, she seemed quite content to settle in for a while.

"Uh…comfy?" he asked.

"I'm so sorry," she said. Pushing against his chest, she twisted, trying to straighten up. That just put her curvy bottom more firmly on his groin, making things worse.

"You're not going anywhere." He slid his arms

around her and rolled onto his side, tugging her with him so they lay facing one another. Their legs were still tangled, their hips and arms met, but the most dangerous zones were at least at a safer distance.

For now.

That didn't mean they'd stay that way, but they had some talking to do first. No way was he letting his pal Woody show up to the party until he made damn sure she knew what she was doing and wanted it just as badly. Not to mention making sure she'd set her plastic coworker straight about where things stood.

"I'm so sorry," she said. "I'm not as clumsy as you must think."

"Yeah, you are. But that's okay," he said.

She wriggled again. "I should go."

"Calm down, I'm not Michael Myers."

Even in the darkness, he could see the whites of her eyes as they grew round as yo-yos. "How did you..."

"Your TV's pretty loud. I recognized theme from the *Halloween* movies."

"I like scary movies."

"Well, they obviously don't scare you."

"Sure they do."

He rolled his eyes. "No way. If they did, you wouldn't have come out here, in the dark, all alone, forgetting a flashlight, wearing just a robe."

He glanced down at her body, unable to resist devouring her with his stare. His eyes had adjusted to the low lighting in the porch and he was able to see her very well. He'd seen enough of her naked that his memory filled in now, reminding him of what was under her clothes. As for the parts he'd never seen…well, his imagination was doing a pretty good job with that.

She was definitely wearing the same robe. But during her fall, it had come uncinched, and gaped open. Beneath it, Mimi wore the skimpiest, sexiest little excuse for a nightgown he'd ever seen. The shoulder straps were two thin strips of lace, which held up a few triangles of satin that strained to contain her breasts. A filmy bit of a skirt fell to about her hips and there it ended. He saw a bit of elastic at her hip and knew she had on another of those thongs. All he'd have to do was bend his arms and he'd be able to fill his hands with two perfect curves of her bottom, as he had earlier when he'd been exploring her so thoroughly.

He wanted the gown off her. He might have seen her most intimate places up close and deliciously personal, but he had yet to lay eyes on what he could already tell were a pair of perfect breasts. He desperately wanted to cup them, taste them, suck her nipples and see if she cooed the way she did when he sucked her clit.

Then again, maybe it was just as well he couldn't. Seeing the rest of her would be like not only inviting Woody to the party, but asking him to burst out and surprise them both. If she so much as flashed a nipple, his cock would be standing up and doing the Macarena. He'd already decided they needed to clear the air before they went back for another round, and the air couldn't be cleared if his southern brain was in charge of the entire conversation.

Still, he couldn't bring himself to stop looking at her, not when he'd been asking himself for hours if she could possibly have been as incredibly sexy as he remembered her being. Answer: no. She was even more so.

Her eyes obviously hadn't adjusted as well as his yet, because she didn't appear to notice the fact that the guy holding her so easily in his arms was in danger of drowning her with his own drool.

"Women in those movies always end up wearing something teeny-tiny at some point," she pointed out.

"Mmm. True. But if you were the heroine, and you'd fallen onto a strange guy you barely knew, you'd have leaped right up, slapped his face and declared you were staying a virgin until at least the fourth sequel."

"Silly—the heroine never makes it to the fourth sequel. By that point, she's too big a star and the movie's being made for the straight-to-DVD set with B actors."

Ahh, a horror-movie aficionado. "Also true."

"But you are right, the ones who sleep around do usually get sliced and diced, don't they?"

"Yep. So do the man-whores."

She chuckled softly. "Is that what you are?"

He didn't laugh, taking the moment to move the conversation where it needed to go. "No. I'm not. I am actually pretty picky when it comes to stuff like…this."

Her lips parted and she moistened them with her pink tongue. "Like this?"

"Yeah, Mimi. Like this. You and me."

"Oh." She was silent for a moment, then whispered, "I've been telling myself I can't have you."

He stiffened.

"It's like there are two halves of me, waging this internal battle about whether or not I can let this happen."

"Which side's winning?" he asked, lazily stroking

her hip, letting his fingertips glide across the high curve of her butt.

"Well, we certainly know which side won this afternoon."

"That wasn't one side of your brain or the other," he assured her. "Something else made that call."

Her libido.

"Yeah, tell me about it." She edged closer, until he could feel her warm breath falling against his bare chest. "I can't seem to be reasonable where you're concerned."

"Reason's overrated," he told her, brushing his mouth gently against her temple. He dropped a hand across her waist, pulling her a little closer, noting how easy, how soft and slow and right this was. They were melting together, totally in sync, and had barely even touched yet. Because this was just what was supposed to happen, he knew it.

"Your brain doesn't have to call the shots entirely," he told her, needing to get this said, "but there is one thing you have to decide."

"What's that?"

He stared into her face, hoping she would hear his seriousness. "Whether or not you have a boyfriend. Is it over?"

She tilted her head back to look up at him, her startling eyes almost a midnight-blue in this shadowy lighting. She heard. She understood. She silently acknowledged the wall between them that was going to stay there until she blew it down with a simple decision that was, after this afternoon, definitely overdue.

Finally, slowly and deliberately, she declared, "I don't, and it's definitely over."

Relief flooded through him. That was all she needed to say. Whatever she'd said to Dimitri, whatever she'd explained to her father, however she'd justified it, she'd made her choice.

"But I have to admit," she added, her voice a little thick, "I am on the lookout for a lover."

The wicked way she lifted one brow told him exactly who she had in mind.

"Does that mean you were inside checking out your own ass in that thong before you came out here to try seducing me?"

Gasping, she tried to sit up. "I swear I had no idea you were here!"

He grabbed her even as he rolled onto his back, and tugged her back down. "I'm kidding."

She landed right on top of him…and stayed there. Her laughter faded, and so did the last bit of her resistance. Something had shifted. The mood, certainly, had gone from playful to serious to sultry. But there was something in her eyes and in her smile, a wildness, a sense of determination.

He suddenly realized what it was.

Mimi had been holding back on her own desires for quite a while—since before they'd met, he would imagine. Now she was going to give them free rein.

She knew what she wanted. She wanted him.

And she was about to show him just how much.

8

IF SOMEONE HAD TOLD her eight days ago that she would be lying here, outside, preparing to make love with the kind of man she'd only ever fantasized about, Mimi would have laughed in his face. Because, eight days ago, she had been quite sure of what her immediate future looked like.

No, she hadn't resigned herself to the inevitability of ending up with Dimitri, no matter how much her father had wanted it. But she had certainly been considering the possibility. And if she had never met Xander, she almost certainly would have at least gone to bed with Dimitri, just to know, absolutely, one hundred percent for sure, whether they could have been right for one another.

Now she knew. The answer was no, they weren't. It hadn't taken going to bed with him; it had just taken someone else showing her he could make her forget any other man existed.

Looking down at Xander, stunned, as always, by his sexy masculinity, she paused to acknowledge that she'd reached one of those pivotal moments in her life.

A before-and-after moment. There was the Mimi who had existed before becoming this man's lover, and the one she would be after tonight. No matter whatever else happened in the future, she had no doubt—none, zero—that this decision would live on in her memories forever.

"Come here," he ordered, reaching up and sinking his hands in her hair.

She let him pull her down, needing to taste him. Their mouths met, softly, more tenderly than they ever had before, as if they were kissing for the first time.

Mimi parted her lips, gently flicking her tongue against his, savoring his taste. Still cupping her head, Xander tilted his to the side, fitting their mouths together more perfectly. They fell into sync, their tongues mating slowly, swirling, thrusting and receding, giving and taking. It was the kind of kiss that could go on for hours and be almost enough in and of itself.

But she knew there would be more. Tonight, they'd have everything.

Slowly ending the kiss, Mimi pushed against his chest and sat up. She lowered both her legs to the sides of the chaise until her toes brushed the cement floor and she was straddling his thighs. Xander didn't attempt to stop her, letting her take control, set the pace. He seemed perfectly happy to lie below her, looking up at her, waiting to see what, exactly, she wanted to do to him.

"I've been thinking about this for days," she admitted through a tight throat.

"Me, too. I wanted to break the wall down last Friday night when I thought you'd gone through with it and brought Mr. Perfect home with you."

"I couldn't…in fact, to be totally honest, I forgot."

A deep laugh erupted from his mouth. "You forgot you had planned to have sex with him? Wow. Talk about an ego killer. I think I'd have to slit my wrists if I ever heard you say that about me."

She shook her head. "That could never happen." Looking down at him and seeing the rock-hard erection bursting against the front seam of his shorts, she struggled to breathe, to stay coherent and said, "Never."

She reaffirmed that to herself when he shifted restlessly beneath her, and she realized he was so huge the thick head of his cock had pushed up and out of the top of his shorts. She'd known he was big, broad and hard everywhere else. But this…well, the sight left her gasping.

"Wow," she whispered, glad she was sitting down as the image of taking all that male strength inside her invaded her mind. Her legs would never have held her.

"Let me see you," he ordered.

"You've seen most of me," she reminded him.

"Not nearly enough. I don't know that I'll ever get enough." He lifted a hand, tracing a path up her side, to the bottom curve of her breast. Swirling the tip of one finger over her nipple, he added, "I really want to see this. I've been fantasizing about your breasts—how they look, how they taste."

Filled with self-confidence fueled by his obvious desire for her, Mimi let the loose robe fall completely off her shoulders. It puddled around her hips on his legs.

Xander watched her in silence, his dark eyes gleaming, narrowing with appreciation. Her breasts were heavy, aching. Against the lace, her nipples were twin pebbles of sensation. She could tell by the way he looked there and drew in an audible, ragged breath, that he was dying to explore all the curves of her body that had been denied to him thus far.

She liked the need he couldn't disguise. Liked how desperately he wanted her. It seemed only fair considering how incredibly hungry she was for him.

"Oh, yes," he groaned when she reached up and slid the strap of her gown off her shoulder.

Mimi held her arm against her body, preventing the fabric from falling away. His brow furrowed, but she intentionally tormented him, knowing how good anticipation could be.

She reached for the other strap, pushing it off, as well. Then she lifted her hand to her breast, pulling at the nightie, peeling it away to reveal herself. An inch of skin, a plump curve…finally, a puckered, upturned nipple, pink and pouty, a bundle of nerve endings just waiting for his intimate attention.

"Beautiful," he said, sounding reverent. He reached up to cup her, and the sensation of his cool, strong hand against her heated skin made her quiver and arch toward his touch.

He didn't wait for her to reveal her other breast, merely reaching up and tearing the silky fabric away himself. She sensed patience wasn't his strongest suit, and she liked that, too.

"Stumbling in on you bottomless was amazing," he said. "If you'd been topless, too, I would have thought I'd landed in heaven."

He caught her other breast in his hand, tweaking the nipple, rolling it between his fingers. Mimi cried out, feeling the touch on her breasts, but also feeling it everywhere else.

When he moved to replace one hand with his mouth, she grabbed his shoulders, digging her nails into the thick, rippling muscle, holding on tight. He breathed over her sensitive skin for a moment, preparing her, then flicked out his tongue.

"Xander," she cried, instinctively arching toward his waiting mouth.

He gave her what she needed, covering her nipple, kissing it, then sucking. Deep. Fast. Hard.

She jerked against him, clutching tight, loving the intensity of it. He was claiming her, every pull of his mouth a demand that she give herself over to him completely.

She hadn't even considered doing anything else.

He played with her breasts for several long moments, teasing one nipple, then moving to the other, always tweaking and stroking whichever one he wasn't suckling. Her hips were rocking now, rubbing against him, edging up his body so she could gain some relief from that strong ridge of masculine flesh that threatened to burst through his gym shorts. The pressure was incredible—a mixture of bliss and torment as the tension rose and she drew closer to the climax that remained tantalizingly out of reach.

He seemed to understand, to know exactly what she needed. Because without a word, he put his big, powerful hands around her waist, and began sliding her up his body. At the same time, he shifted down. And down.

"No way, twice in one day is just selfish," she muttered when she realized what he intended to do.

"Shut up."

She shut up. Xander seemed intent on going right back to where they'd left off earlier today. He moved down far enough on the chaise so that she was sitting on his chest.

And then he moved a little farther.

She came immediately. He hadn't even needed to push her dripping wet thong out of the way, he'd merely covered her mound with his mouth, flicked his tongue against the satin material, and the top of her head had blown off.

Tears rose to her eyes, the relief was so great, the bliss so immense. Before she'd even had time to fully process it, Xander was ripping her panties off, tearing them down the side, throwing them to the ground.

"Uh-uh, my turn," she said when he moved his mouth toward her sex again.

"But I want it."

She chuckled, hearing the boyish, pleading tone in his voice.

"Have I told you yet that I love oral sex?" he asked.

"I kinda got that," she murmured as she scooted back, so very thankful for the chaise, which was the perfect height and width. Straddling him, letting her moist, soft opening scrape across him as she worked her way down his body, was a delightful torment for them both.

When she reached his hips, she brushed herself against the tip of his erection, then climbed off him. "Most times when men say that, they mean they like getting it."

"I like getting it *and* giving it," he admitted, watching her closely as she bent to her knees beside the chaise.

She didn't taste him immediately, wanting to see him first, to gauge whether he could possibly be as big as she suspected he was. Her hands shook when she lifted them to the waistband of his gym shorts. She traced the tip of her finger across the bulbous head of his cock, hearing him hiss in reaction.

"Mimi…"

"Shh. My turn."

Her finger was wet with his body's essence, and she lifted it to her mouth, sampling the salty flavor of him. He reached down and tangled his hand in her hair, never taking his eyes off her.

Hungry for more, she began to work his shorts down, carefully, lifting them over that throbbing ridge of flesh. She let her hand brush against him, watching his rippling stomach muscles flex in reaction. Holding her breath, she drew the shorts all the way down, revealing inch after glorious inch of him.

"Oh. My. God," she whispered, needing to take a moment to stare at the male beauty before her. She inhaled, but her breath didn't seem to reach her lungs; she felt dizzy, light-headed. So weak with desire she had the urge to climb up and impale herself on him now, right now, without any further delays.

But she also wanted to taste him. To pleasure him the way he'd pleasured her. So she leaned closer, close enough to brush her lips across the head.

"Hey, Mimi," he said with a deep, guttural groan, "remember how I said I like to give it and to get it?"

"Mmm-hmm."

"I really like them both at the same time."

He moved quickly, not warning her what he was about to do. Before she knew it, he'd reached down, put his hands around her waist and pulled her up onto him, her mouth still near his massive erection, his on her… "Oh, yes!"

He dove into her, but this time, she didn't have to just helplessly take it. She was able to act, as well. She licked another drop of moisture off the tip of his cock, then widened her mouth and took him in it, sucking hard.

The pleasure was exquisite. He was playing her body like an instrument, even as she took pure joy in tasting and sucking him into near incoherence. Mimi had never done this before, never had a lover who wanted to do things out of order on the checklist. She could only think whoever had written that checklist needed a mental checkup of his own, because this…was…heaven.

They gave themselves over to the eroticism of it for a few wonderful minutes, during which she came again so hard she sobbed. Then Xander gently moved out from under her, dropping to his knees on the patio.

"Gotta be in you now, Mimi," he told her between pants, sounding desperate, on the edge.

She nodded, rolling onto her back. Xander reached for his discarded shorts and grabbed a condom out of the pocket. She didn't even consider teasing him about being so sure he'd need it sooner rather than later, just thankful he had it.

He sheathed himself, then bent to kiss her again. His tongue thrust deep, and she tasted herself on him, but didn't care. That was right, and good and perfect, and things like shyness or modesty had absolutely no place between them. Not anymore.

"Please," she whispered, "I need you."

"I know what you need."

She remembered his words to her about knowing what she needed and how she needed it. Never had that been more true than right now.

She raised her arms, intending to draw him down. But instead, he pulled her up until she was sitting on the edge of the chaise, her legs parted, her sex swollen and so ready.

Holding her hips, he moved closer, until his cock was nestled against the lips of her sex. He stroked, moistening himself with her body's juices, then began to slide into her, with wonderful—agonizing—restraint.

She held her breath, looking down, watching him slowly penetrate her, stunned by the beauty of *them.* It was wanton and earthy, so primal and perfect.

She was feeling stretched and wonderfully full before he was even halfway home. Urging him on with whimpers and whispered pleas, she wrapped her legs around his hips, trying to pull him forward, to take and take and take.

And finally, he gave. He groaned her name, caught her mouth in a hard kiss and plunged deep.

She let out a tiny scream, but he swallowed it with his kiss. They didn't move for a moment, and she sensed he was savoring the sensations, as she was. Then, finally, he drew out a little, enough for her to miss the heat of him, before plunging again.

"Yes, more," she pleaded, needing him to go faster, to thrust and pound, to empty and fill her, to leave his mark deep within her, where nobody had ever touched her before.

"Amazing," he muttered, "you feel amazing." He kissed her jaw, moved to her neck, sucked her nape. And continued to stroke, slow then hard, shallow then deep.

She tangled her hands in his hair, kissed him where she could, pushed to meet every thrust, pulled to take when he teased her by withholding one.

Finally, she saw the way his muscles were bunching and his lip curled up into a near snarl. He was close to the edge.

"Come in me, do it, finish it," she demanded.

He growled something, then, revealing unbelievable strength, grabbed her bottom and pulled her off the chair. He didn't even stop making love to her as he somehow rose to his feet, carrying her with him. Mimi held on, dizzy, dazzled and dazed.

"I want you in a bed," he told her.

"Are you crazy?"

He pushed into her harder, daring her to think he couldn't do exactly what he'd set out to do. And somehow, he did manage to stay inside her, his arms curled under her bottom, as he bent over and went through the secret door that led to his room. She was torn between laughing and screaming at him to make her come again as he moved through the tiny closet into his own bedroom.

When they reached the big bed, he lowered her onto it and followed her down, she realized she didn't want to laugh or scream. She wanted to sigh, to cry with happiness. Because sinking into the bed, with him on top of her, being able to look up and see his handsome face in the softly lit room, in a soft, comfortable bed, was exactly how she wanted to finish this night.

The frenzy died a little, as if that's what he'd been going for, and Xander slowed his strokes. Bracing himself on one arm, he moved a hand to her breast, stroking her gently, almost reverently. "You're perfect," he told her.

"This is perfect," she replied. And she meant it. *Sheer perfection.*

She might not have even realized it was possible a couple of weeks ago. Now she knew it was. He'd shown her.

And, she realized, he intended to continue to show her.

All night long.

DESPITE NOT HAVING drifted to sleep until at least 3:00 a.m., after hours of the most incredible sex of his life, Xander woke up at eight feeling better than he ever had. It had taken him a second to remember everything that had happened, but hearing Mimi's contented sigh, and feeling her long, slim leg slide between his as she draped herself over him in her sleep, everything had come flooding back.

He would love to stay this way, all tangled up, the sheets long gone, the warmth of their bodies all they needed. But he had somewhere to be, and had to get up. That meant he had to get her up. Because he didn't intend to let her out of his sight today—so she was coming with him.

"Hey, beautiful," he whispered against her cheek, "are you hungry?"

She mumbled something.

"What was that?"

"Hungry for you," she repeated.

His mouth watered. He was hungry for her, too, and suspected he always would be.

He couldn't get enough of her, despite having made love to her for hour after hour the previous night. Hell, he hadn't even realized he was capable of staying hard for so long, or coming a gallon at a time. He just knew that all Mimi had to do was flash him a tiny, flirtatious smile, and he wanted to crawl all over her.

"I meant," he said, knowing he had no time to act on those kinds of thoughts right now, "are you hungry for breakfast?"

She yawned widely, finally opening her eyes to peer at him through long, tangled strands of red hair. "Didn't we eat at around two o'clock this morning?"

"That was dessert," he replied. He reached out and rubbed a tiny brown smear on her cheek. "Missed a spot of chocolate."

She nipped at his finger. "That ice cream was cold."

"Not after you warmed it up with your body." He sighed, remembering licking spoonfuls of sweet, creamy confection off her nipples, her thighs, her clit.

"I'm just glad you didn't have Chunky Monkey in your freezer," she said with a giggle. "You might never have found all the chunks."

He leered. "I don't know. I think if I looked closely enough, I'd have gotten every last nut." Then, knowing she was about to seduce him back into her arms, he leaped off the bed and swatted her gorgeous backside.

She glared.

"Come on, time to get something to eat."

"In bed?"

"Nope."

She wagged her brows. "Are you sure you don't want to have breakfast in bed?"

No, he wasn't sure. He desperately wanted to get back in that bed and not get up again until dinnertime. But he had obligations. "Come on…fluffy pancakes, crispy bacon. I'm cooking. You know you want it."

She perked right up. "I am starving. I worked up an appetite last night. Do you have everything you need to make it?"

"Yep, it's all covered." He headed for the bathroom. "Come on, take a shower with me and we'll go."

She paused halfway out of the bed. "Go? I thought you were cooking."

"I am, just not here," he told her as he turned on the shower, glad his big, old-fashioned claw-foot tub was big enough for two. He'd like to make it a long, sultry shower—and someday wanted to see Mimi soaking in this tub, up to her chin in bubbles. But for now, a quick wash would have to do.

"Okay, mister, what's going on?" she asked as she joined him in the bathroom.

"Pancake breakfast at work," he told her with a grin. "It's a fundraiser. I'm on KP duty from nine 'til eleven. So get moving, woman."

Her jaw dropped. "At the fire station?"

"No, the gas station…of course the fire station! You in?"

He waited, wondering what she'd do. He hadn't given a second thought to inviting the Mimi who'd spent the night in his arms to join him at a community breakfast, where there would be lots of families, other firefighters and locals.

But the trust-fund Mimi? The one born with the silver spoon in her mouth, whose father owned one of the biggest independent grocery store chains in the south, who'd been taken to some snazzy, ritzy restaurant just a few nights ago by her snazzy, ritzy ex? Well, he hadn't even been thinking about her when he issued the invitation.

He should have, he knew that. That other woman was part of Mimi, too. And someday the two parts of her were going to have to come together.

He didn't worry about that day, though. Because Xander had already realized that, no matter what the outward trappings, or even excluding the crazy-wild lust they'd shared the night before, there really was only one Mimi when all was said and done. The Mimi he'd come to know smiled easily, laughed brightly, would climb a tree to rescue a cat for a kid she didn't know. She would brave scary-movie psycho-killers to retrieve forgotten scissors so that same kid couldn't possibly get hurt on them the next day—he'd gotten the scissors during the night when he'd gone out to retrieve his shorts and the remnants of her nightgown. She was witty and honest, easygoing and fun, sexy as hell and a little bit klutzy.

She was not the kind of woman who would turn up her nose at a firehouse pancake breakfast. At least, he hoped not.

She proved his faith in her by offering him a big smile. "So am I going to get to meet your firefighter buddies and hear all about your bad-boy ways?"

Allowing himself the tiniest sigh of relief, he chuckled. "Sorry, I'm the new guy, they barely know me. I've only been there a month. Not enough time to be really bad."

"I'm sure you could manage if you try," she said with a suggestive lift of her brow.

"I think I proved that last night."

"Was that you being bad? I would have called that very—*very*—good."

"Right back at you," he growled.

Their mouths met in a kiss, but Xander didn't let himself get lost in it. He ended it with one lingering caress of her hip, turning back to the tub.

"So if you've been there a month, where were you staying before you moved in here last weekend?" she asked, watching as he tested the water.

"An extended-stay hotel."

Her eyes widened. "Seriously?"

"Yep. I didn't know anybody, had no idea where I'd end up when I got on the road from Chicago and drove down here to start the job."

Holding the curtain back, he gestured for her to get in ahead of him, holding her hand while she stepped over the high-sided tub into the steamy stream of water.

"That was quite a change," she said as he joined her.

"Which was exactly what I was going for."

"Why?"

Seeing the curiosity in her eyes, he thought about how to explain. He wasn't certain he could convey how badly he'd needed to completely break away from his old life, to start a new one, where there were no tragic memories, no lingering melancholy over the things he'd lost, and regret over all the things he would never have.

He'd known for a long time that his future kids would probably grow up not knowing their grandmother. But it had never crossed his mind that fate could be so cruel as to deprive him of his father, too, who'd been so strong and healthy—right up until the day he hadn't been.

"Xander?"

He still hesitated. This wasn't exactly typical morning-after conversation. They should be talking about how amazing the night had been, how he felt sure he'd never experienced anything more incredible than being wrapped in her tight, hot body.

But something made him talk, open up to her, in a way he hadn't with anyone else since he'd found out his dad had cancer sixteen months ago.

"I told you my parents died last year," he finally said, reaching for the soap and gently rubbing it over her bare shoulders.

"Yes." Her wide eyes looked moist, and not just from the steam. "That must have been so painful."

"It fucking sucked," he told her. There was no other way to put it. "I missed them, of course." He swallowed, hard. "It was bad with my mom, but somehow even worse with my dad, who actually moved in with me when he got really sick. So I was with him almost nonstop at the end."

"That's also a blessing, isn't it?" she asked. "That you had so much time with him?"

He nodded. It hadn't felt like much of a blessing then, watching the once proud, strong, virile man—who'd also been a firefighter all his life—succumb to a disease that had eaten him from the inside out in a matter of weeks. Now, though, remembering the moments they'd had, the opportunity Xander had been given to thank his old man for all he'd done for him over the years, he knew Mimi was right.

He reached for the shampoo bottle and squeezed a dollop of gooey liquid into his hand. Her hair was so beautiful, and the idea of washing it so intimate. He just couldn't resist, loving the way it glided through his fingers as he smoothed the shampoo over the long tresses.

"So you were looking for a change, a way to get away from the memories?"

He nodded, focused on her hair, but also let himself open up in a way he hadn't expected to. "I was also looking to get away from the future I'd always imagined...but no longer had to look forward to."

She gazed up at him, her lips trembling. "You have a future to look forward to," she insisted.

"I know that. I just needed to make myself see the alternative one, instead of the one I'd always imagined. And I guess I felt like the only way I was going to stop feeling like crap about losing my entire family in the space of six months was to go far away. Create something new rather than trying to stay and rebuild on the ashes of what was gone."

A tear spilled out of the corner of her eye.

He cleared his throat, uncomfortable. "I wasn't playing the sympathy card."

"I know that." She took the soap from his hand, rolling it between hers, then lifting the suds to his chest. Washing him gently, she swayed closer, murmuring,

"I'm sorry you went through everything you did. But I can't deny I'm glad you ended up here."

"Me, too."

She leaned her head back, rinsing out her hair, then moved out of the way for him to do the same. He'd thought they were finished with their previous conversation, but she was apparently still curious.

"So tell me about your parents. What's your best memory from childhood?"

"We always had two Christmases," he told her, laughing softly, surprising even himself.

"Lucky!"

"My mom was Greek Orthodox, my dad Irish Catholic. Double holidays were a standard. And since I was an only kid…"

"Oh, I know those only-child Christmases," she said with a laugh. "I'm pretty sure I have a couple thousand Beanie Babies boxed up in my parents' attic to this day."

Their laughter hit Xander right in the heart. The tight, painful squeeze he always felt when talking about his parents eased a bit, thanks to Mimi's smile and her sweetness. Something seemed to open in him. He found himself remembering special moments and being able to laugh at them again. He also liked listening to her own stories of her rich, pushy father, and her sweet-natured mother, who apparently really ran the house but liked to let her husband think he did.

Sounded like the secret of all successful marriages; his parents' had been the same.

By the time they'd finished showering, he felt almost buoyant, all trace of melancholy gone. Because of her.

"Ouch—eight-thirty," he said spying the clock in

his bedroom as they got out and dried off. "We'd better hurry."

Mimi slipped into her robe. "Do you think I'll have a better chance getting back into my place unseen if I go by way of your closet, to the patio, to my closet, or if I just dash across the hall between our front doors?"

He glanced out the window. It was a bright, sunny morning, and he'd already heard Mr. Leadfoot clomping around upstairs. If Tuck were at all like Xander had been at that age, he'd be outside exploring his new neighborhood.

"I'd go for the front hall. It's quicker," he told her. Then he eyed her wet hair, her damp face—beautiful without a drop of makeup—and asked, "This might be the worst question you can ask a woman, but can you be ready in fifteen minutes?"

She smirked. "You have no idea. I am the queen of oversleeping and racing out the door. Time me."

Without another word, she spun around and hurried out of his bedroom. He followed her. "Want me to make sure the coast is clear?" he asked. Xander didn't care who knew he was involved with Mimi, but he also knew she was very close to Anna and Obi-Wan. She might not want them knowing the truth of their relationship just yet. Whatever that relationship might be.

Good. That was all he needed to know about it right now. It was good.

"Thanks," she said, watching as he opened the door and stuck his head out.

He glanced up the stairs, down the hallway and out the front. "All clear," he said once he'd made sure nobody was in sight.

"Here I go."

She slipped out, her robe clutched tightly around her naked body, and darted the few steps to her door.

Only to get there, lift a hand to the knob, then drop it and turn around with a definite eye-roll. "I don't have my keys."

Snickering, he muttered, "Foiled again. Some supersleuth you are."

"Don't make fun of me or you'll lose your date for the pancake breakfast."

"Come on, you know you're dying to taste my bacon."

She wagged her eyebrows. "Or your sausage."

"As long as you remember it's thick kielbasa and not Vienna," he retorted, laughing as she walked back to him, directly into his arms, as if she knew that's where she belonged.

She opened her mouth to reply, but a noise from above distracted her. They both looked up, just in time to see a curly-haired brunette begin to descend the stairs from above. With her was Tuck, the cat-lover, who was saucer-eyeing them.

No wonder. Mimi had on a skimpy robe. Xander had a towel slung around his hips and nothing else. And they were embracing in the public hallway.

"Oh, sorry," the woman whispered, immediately turning and trying to turn her son, as well.

The boy resisted, bouncing on his toes to try to look over his petite mother's shoulder when she blocked him with her body.

Mimi's face erupted in flames. "I locked myself out," she said. She hadn't lied…but she didn't elaborate, either. Of course, considering the way they were dressed, and that she had been wrapped in his arms until a second ago, when she'd quickly stepped away from him before they scarred the six-year-old for life, the woman had to know the truth.

"Do you need me to get my father to bring you a spare key?" she asked.

"I bet I could pick the lock!" said Tuck, who was still trying to peek around at them.

"Uh, no, thank you," Mimi said, edging closer to Xander's open doorway. "I'm going to go through the screen porch to the secret door. I'll be fine."

The brunette smiled a little, and a twinkle appeared in her pretty eyes. "Are you sure your other door is unlocked?"

Mimi chewed a hole in her lip as she slowly nodded. "Pretty sure."

"Okay then. Talk to you later," she said. "Come on, Tuck, I forgot something."

"What'd you forget?"

"My big bag of none'ya."

"Aww, Mom…"

"It's none'ya business, now let's go."

Mimi and Xander went back inside, both of them chuckling at how the young mother dealt with her inquisitive son.

"That was pretty embarrassing," he said. "Thank goodness I remembered the towel."

"And thank goodness I had the robe," she replied with a sigh, already heading for his room, so she could make use of the secret exit. "Imagine if I'd tried to make a naked dash!"

"That was Anna and Obi-Wan's daughter, right?"

"Yes, Helen, we met last night, after you'd left," she said. Then she stopped, midstep. "Oh, wow, she's going to think I'm a total skank-ho."

"That's ridiculous."

"She saw me with Dimitri last night, and I know she figured he was my..."

"But he's not," he interjected.

She didn't look consoled. "As far as she knows, we could have be seriously involved."

"But you aren't." He put his hands on her waist, squeezing tight. "Stop beating yourself up, all right? You and I know the truth about how nonserious you really were, and Dimitri knows it, too. You didn't break any hearts when you broke up with him...and we *all* know that."

She looked away, still obviously uncomfortable.

"It'll be fine. I promise."

She took a deep breath, then finally nodded. But instead of leaving right away, she tilted her head to the side, as if she'd just remembered something. "It was kind of kind of interesting last night when Helen arrived. Dimitri and my father were still here."

She quickly told him about the way Plastic Man had reacted to seeing Helen. Sounded to him like Mr. Smooth had a few secrets in his past. "I'm sorry, I can't picture him with someone like that. She's so...sweet."

"And I'm not?" she asked, not sounding at all offended. She liked being naughty—spicy—for him. And he liked indulging her naughtiness.

"You're sweet, babe. You're very sweet."

"Oh…so you *can* picture him with me?" she asked, looking coy, as if trying to make him jealous.

It worked. Big-time. He grabbed her around the waist and pulled her close. "Don't even think about it."

"I haven't," she promised, twining her arms around his neck. "Not since the night you fell out of my closet like the world's biggest, hottest jack-in-the-box."

"And you were the world's sexiest pantiless home invader."

"My home," she reminded him again.

"Yeah, yeah." Glancing at the clock, and seeing how little time they had left, he pushed her toward the closet. "Okay, wow me. You've got five minutes."

"A lot can happen in five minutes," she said suggestively.

"Like you maybe getting some clothes on?"

"If you insist," she said.

Then, with another quick kiss on his lips and a smile that exuded happiness, she ducked into the closet and disappeared.

9

OVER THE NEXT few days, Mimi found herself balancing the pressure of her increasingly stressful job with the wonderfully exciting, happy moments to which she was able to escape at night. Not every night, unfortunately—Xander had a couple of double shifts when he'd had to stay at the station. But at least Monday night and Wednesday night she'd been able to go to sleep in his arms again, as she had Saturday. Each morning after, she had woken up to watch him sleeping beside her, once again amazed that she could have found him so suddenly and fallen for him so fast.

He was becoming an addiction.

Every minute she spent with him was both a gift and a revelation. For a man who insisted he was nothing special, just a regular guy, he always managed to surprise her. Each time they were together, he would invariably say something that shocked her, made her think or made her laugh. After she'd had a really crappy day on Monday, including a big fight with the manager of the printing company who did all the Burdette Foods sales circulars, he had insisted on rubbing her shoulders. He'd then gone out for pizza and had come back with a bouquet of flowers, probably purchased off the back of a roadside truck, but so pretty and genuine, she'd felt all blubbery.

There was really only one fly in the ointment, one thing that had kept her from diving headfirst into the bliss of this completely unexpected—and ever-so-welcome—love affair.

Dimitri.

She'd headed to work Monday knowing there were quite a lot of things on her to-do list. First was a weekly staff meeting with her employees. Then she had a conference call with some of her out-of-state counterparts. Then a lunch meeting. Then an evaluation of several bids from new printers they were considering using for their in-store circulars, since their current one had been slipping up a little too often lately.

And somewhere in there, she'd intended to find a minute with Dimitri to make sure he knew they were no longer dating.

She'd made it fairly clear Saturday evening. She'd come right out and said they were in no way serious, reiterating that they'd only gone out "a couple of times." He should absolutely have been able to read between the lines. But the words *I don't want to go out with you again* hadn't actually left her mouth, and she'd feel a lot better once they did.

She hadn't been lying to Xander Saturday night when she'd told him she wasn't involved with Dimitri anymore, especially since she'd barely been involved with him to begin with. Because in her mind, she wasn't involved, not in any way, emotionally or physically. That was absolutely without a doubt.

But she hadn't really thought about the need to have the conversation until Xander said something that told her he assumed she already had. When he'd mentioned that she hadn't broken Dimitri's heart when she broke up with him—which would be the truth, she knew—she realized Xander believed she'd already had some kind of final scene with the other man.

Which was exactly what she'd wanted to have on Monday. Only, when she'd arrived at work, she'd learned there had literally been a fire at one of their stores down in Jacksonville, and Dimitri had left suddenly, going down there to put out the proverbial ones that had come after it. So she hadn't seen him for three days.

It hadn't seemed like a conversation to have over the phone, not that they'd spoken more than once, and that mostly about business. So the pressure had mounted. By now, Thursday, she just wanted to get it over with. Which was why she was so relieved when she got to work that morning and found out he was back and in a meeting with her father.

She dropped off her things at her desk, finished signing a few documents, returned a call, then prepared to go to her dad's office and join them. She intended to ask Dimitri to lunch, fully expecting to clear the air. Then she could go home to Xander tonight without anything weighing on her mind, her heart or her conscience.

But before she could do anything, her office door opened, and her assistant, Lauren, popped her head in. "Hey, boss, got a sec?"

About Mimi's age, Lauren was bright, quick-thinking, and was Mimi's right-hand man. If not for the fact that Mimi was her supervisor, she suspected she and Lauren could be very good friends. As it was, they got along perfectly, and did as much as they could socially without crossing any boss/employee lines.

"Sure, how's everything going?" Suddenly remembering her assistant's request for some time off, she asked, "Wait, your high school reunion's not this weekend, is it?"

Lauren waved a hand. "No, that's not until next month. I wanted to talk to you about something else."

"What's up?" she asked, gesturing for the other woman to sit down.

Lauren dropped to a chair on the opposite side of Mimi's desk. "God, I hate Thursdays. They're so close to the weekend...but they always seem to go on forever."

"I don't know, I think Monday has it beat in terms of worst day," she said with a chuckle. Monday had been particularly hard this week, since she'd had the kind of weekend she'd wanted to go on and on and on.

After the pancake breakfast, during which she'd met a lot of very friendly firefighters and their families, she and Xander had gone shopping to stock up his new apartment. She'd taken him to one of her stores, of course, bullying him into using her discount and making him buy more than boxed mac-and-cheese and peanut butter.

Then they'd gone home, unloaded everything...and gone back to bed. They'd gotten up to eat—peanut butter—and gone back to bed, not arising again until the next morning.

It had been the most erotic thirty-six hours of her life. There were things she'd already done with Xander that would have made her blush to even consider doing with anyone else. Things she'd done again Monday night. And last night.

And she wanted to do them again. Soon.

"I, uh…damn, this probably isn't any of my business," Lauren said, sounding uncomfortable.

Really curious, she leaned forward and said, "Tell me what's going on."

Lauren looked at her hands, which were clenched in her lap, then out the window, then down at her hands again.

"Would you spill it? You look like you did that time you had to tell me you'd come back in to work late one night and caught the janitors doing it in the break room."

"Ha. I wish it were something that simple."

Simple? The two janitors in question had both been in their sixties, both married and both men. There had been nothing simple about that situation.

To give her credit, Lauren had had the presence of mind—and the feisty temperament—to order them to get their clothes back on, and not to leave until they'd bleached down every surface in the break room. Despite that, neither Mimi nor Lauren had eaten a single lunch in there since.

She wondered if either of the men were still married. Or still hiding in their very clean closets.

Lauren's next comment killed any curiosity Mimi might have about anybody else's marital status.

"I think Dimitri's going to propose to you."

Her jaw fell and she sagged back in the chair. *"What?"*

Though they hadn't broadcast it, Lauren knew Mimi and Dimitri had been dating. She also knew—and had felt confident enough in her relationship with Mimi to comment about it—that they weren't right for each other. Lauren called Dimitri the Stud Stick. Probably with good reason.

"Tell me you're joking."

"Nope, I'm not. Believe me, if I thought this was good news, that you wanted to hear it and would give even a minute's thought to accepting, I would never have said a word. I'm not a proposal spoiler…that's just mean."

"You're right. I don't want to hear it, and I wouldn't give a minute's thought to it." She swiped a hand through her hair, knocking it out of its bun but not caring. "I'd been planning to tell him today that I didn't even want to go out with him anymore."

"Obviously he thinks everything's hunky-dory." She shook her head woefully. "Lord, what fools these men can be."

"How could he possibly think I'd be interested in a proposal? Hell, we're not even involved, we've never…" She flushed, realizing she was saying too much.

"Oh, come on, it's not like I don't know you two haven't done the nasty," Lauren said with an eye-roll.

"It's that obvious?"

"You can tell when two people have seen each other naked. And I've never seen a look on your face that says you've seen him wearing anything less than khakis and a J. Crew sweater…nor have you much looked like you cared."

True. All true.

"Heck, I've never seen *anybody* who's acted like they've even seen him with his shirt off."

Hmm. Helen might have. But that wasn't Mimi's business.

"Why do you think he's going to ask me to marry him?"

"Because I came in really early this morning and went to ask your dad a question. From outside his office, I heard him talking to Dimitri about getting your grandmother's ring so it could be reset for you."

That was serious. And wasn't it just like her father to presume to not only talk to a man she was barely dating about his pending proposal, but to also demand he use a Burdette family heirloom, rather than picking out a damn ring himself?

There were times she loved her father and wanted only to get along with him.

There were other times when she came close to reaching for bleach to hide the bloodstains and a shovel to bury the body.

"I'm really sorry, boss," Lauren said. "I know you don't need to deal with this stress right now."

Seeing the genuine concern on the other woman's face, Mimi nodded her thanks.

"I should be used to it. But honestly, I can't believe this is happening," she said, rubbing at the corners of her eyes with the tips of her two fingers.

"Neither can I!" a male voice snapped.

She jerked her head up, shocked to see her father

storming into her office. Dimitri was right behind him, and he shot her a look that was half commiserating, half scolding.

Lauren leapt to her feet. "Excuse me, I need to get back to work."

Though he was usually very polite to all the staff, her father ignored the young woman as she scurried out of the office. Striding right over to Mimi's desk, he slammed his hand—a hand that was holding a brightly colored sales circular—down on top of it.

Mimi stared at it in confusion. "What's wrong?"

"What do you mean what's wrong? Are you trying to say you weren't just talking about this…this… *abomination?*"

A strong word for eight sheets of four-color newsprint.

Confused, she could only shake her head. "I honestly have no idea, Dad. Why don't you calm down, take a seat and tell me what this is all about."

"Her own department, and she has no idea," he snapped, turning to Dimitri.

"Maybe we should fill her in," Dimitri replied, calmly, which was good since her father, the CEO of Burdette Foods, looked ready to blow a gasket.

Whatever had happened, it was serious.

"I wish somebody would," she said, trying to keep her temper in check. She did not like feeling like a kid called on the carpet before her father and judgmental older brother.

Hmm. An older brother. To be honest, when she thought about it, that's kind of how she'd been thinking of Dimitri lately. She liked him, respected him…but sure didn't want to make out with him, and God help the man if he ever actually proposed. She'd be saying no quicker than a sober virgin at a frat party.

Her father threw both hands up in the air and strode across the room to her corner window, which looked out over downtown Athens. She'd taken the smallest executive office just because of that pretty view. Now she kind of wished she could step out of that window and fly away.

Like in her dream.

She'd flown in that amazing dream she'd had the first night when she'd drunk some of Obi-Wan's tea. She'd forgotten it again until just that moment. Which made her wonder if she'd had any other dreams the second time she'd drunk the tea…dreams she couldn't remember, either.

"Let me show you," Dimitri said, bringing her mind back to the tense moment at hand.

Leaning over her desk, he flipped through a few pages of the sales circular, until he came to the page displaying this week's meat specials. Running the tip of his perfectly manicured finger over the photographs of the products, he stopped about halfway down, tapping on one tiny picture and block of text.

Mimi peered at the image. Then, not believing what she was seeing, grabbed her reading glasses that she used when she'd read so much she could barely see anymore, and looked again.

"Oh. My. God."

"Exactly!" her father said.

She understood why he was so angry. Because she was hit with a rush of fury herself.

Right in the middle of the meat ad, between the mention of the buy-one-get-one deal on London Broil, and the special on chicken breasts, was a small hand-drawn image.

"It's a penis," she whispered, still not believing her eyes.

"Of course it's a penis!" her father said.

This was a nightmare.

Whoever had drawn it was talented. It was just about the most realistic cartoon penis and testicles she'd ever seen, right down to some icky purple veins. Nobody could claim it was a mirage seen only by dirty-minded people.

Well-drawn, but small and cleverly concealed. Probably only about a half inch long, it was lost amid all the other images…until you looked close. And to drive the point home, directly beneath it were the teeny-tiny words *Tube Steak! Eat all you want for free!*

She slid her fingers under the glasses, rubbing her eyes again, aware of a headache that had just begun to pound behind them.

What to do...a recall, obviously. Strip all the copies from the stores, publish an apology in the next circular?

"How could you let this happen?" her father barked.

She stiffened. Mimi had been focused on the *what* of the issue, and the *how* to fix it. Not on casting the blame for it happening in the first place. That could come later, after they did some major ass-covering.

But not according to her father.

"Me?"

"You're the head of the marketing and advertising departments, aren't you?" He swung around to face her, his face red, spittle flying from his lips. "If you were anybody but my daughter, I'd fire you on the spot."

If she were anyone but his daughter, she'd tell him to go fuck himself. Because while she was the head of the departments, as he'd said, she was also very good at her job. She had gone over the proofs of that circular with a magnifying glass in hand, like she did every week, and knew damn well that obscenity had not been on it. She had the proof filed away, with her initials on it, and if there was a penis on the damn thing, she would not only tender her resignation on the spot, but she'd also drop to the floor and kiss her father's hand in supplication.

But there wasn't. She knew it down to her very soul.

She had an immediate suspicion about what might have happened. Her fight with their printer, who'd had the contract for so long they'd grown lazy, had blown up last week. She'd told the owner she was putting out a request for proposal for bids from other companies. The man was a good-old-boy redneck with a sexist attitude and a chip on his shoulder, and he had been furious. She couldn't help but wonder if he'd expressed his fury to somebody on his staff, who'd decided to slip a little something extra into the ad. Or, heck, if he'd done it himself!

It made perfect, infuriating sense. But her father didn't even want to hear an explanation—he was busy blaming her.

"I want everyone in those departments in a meeting in one hour," he snapped, crossing his arms over his chest and tapping his foot imperiously. "One of those jokers thought he was being funny and might have cost us a major media firestorm. Well, let's see if he's still laughing when he's standing on the unemployment line."

"It wasn't one of my people...."

"Of course it was. You just don't want to admit it because you treat them like friends instead of employees."

Her jaw fell. "What on earth are you talking about?"

"Oh, I know about your pedicures with that assistant of yours. You can't treat subordinates like gal pals, Mimi, or you get taken advantage of. This obviously proves it."

She couldn't understand what he meant, then something dawned on her. She had given Lauren a gift certificate to a local day spa for a mani/pedi after she'd done a terrific job on a project, and had decided at the last minute to go with her. Dimitri had been taking her out for dinner that night, their very first date, and had heard all about it.

And he'd felt the need to run to tattle to her father.

Like...like a big brother.

She turned her attention to him, glared with such heat he flinched. Her eyes never left his face, though she was addressing her father. "Oh, is that what you've heard?"

Dimitri swiped a hand through his perfect hair, messing it up as much as she'd ever seen it. "Mimi, I..."

"Save it," she snarled, talking not to Dimitri, her colleague, but to Dimitri, the man she'd actually gone out with a couple of times. Had he been reporting the amount of money she spent, where she ate her lunch, or how quickly she'd let him kiss her? Bastard.

Mimi closed her eyes, drew in a deep breath, and grabbed hold of her emotions and her anger with both fists. When she felt under control, she turned back to her father. "Fine. Meeting in your office in one hour." Her eyes narrowing, she added, "But *I* will decide which of my staff members need to be in attendance."

Their stares locked, and she noticed his eyes flared a little. They'd had a few run-ins, but she hadn't ever addressed him with such fury and utter disdain in her voice. But he'd laid the groundwork for this confrontation when he'd stormed in here and thrown around his accusations. Not to mention making that hateful crack about firing her.

The ridiculous thing was, if she were anyone but his daughter, he would have treated her a whole lot more respectfully. At the very least, he would have bothered to ask if she had any idea what had happened, rather than just deciding she'd screwed up.

"Now how about both of you get out so I can get busy figuring out how this happened?"

Her father's stiff, angry posture softened a little, as if he suddenly realized how righteously furious she was. "Mimi…"

"If you'll excuse me, *sir,* I really need to get to work."

He hesitated, his mouth pulling down and his brow furrowing into a puzzled frown. Her dad was the type to bluster and fume, then calm down and listen to reason, which was obviously what was happening here.

Problem was, it was too late. He'd crossed a line this time with his minion's help. She wasn't going to just laugh this off as Dad being Dad. He'd behaved badly, been a lousy manager, and once she cleared her name—and her staff—she was going to make sure he knew exactly how she felt about it.

Beyond that, she honestly didn't know what she was going to do. But if she still felt the way she did right now, it might not be just her staff members walking the unemployment line. Because she'd quit her job before she ever let him make her feel the way he'd made her feel this morning, her future with her family's company be damned.

Part of her was horrified by the very idea, considering she'd been trying so hard to prove herself worthy of the CEO job. Another part—the part that had other dreams and wishes, that sometimes fantasized about going to a new company where she could really push herself creatively—found it incredibly exciting.

Right now, Mimi truly had no idea which way things would go. All she knew was she had sixty minutes to clear her name, and her staff.

After that...the future was wide-open.

THOUGH THEY'D BEEN physically involved for under a week, the moment Xander saw Mimi Thursday evening, he knew something was wrong. Seriously wrong.

It wasn't just the frown on her face. Or the dark circles under her eyes. Or the streaks on her cheeks that told of recently shed tears.

The spoon and half gallon of ice cream in her hand, and the big glass of wine sitting beside her on her kitchen counter said a whole lot, too.

He'd come over right after he'd gotten home from the station, knocking once, then letting himself in after she called out that the door was unlocked. Seeing her in such a wrecked state, his stomach dropped and he went right to her, taking the ice cream out of her hands and pulling her into his arms.

He didn't say anything, and when she opened her mouth to, he stopped her with a kiss.

She dropped the spoon to the floor with a clatter, then lifted her hands up to encircle his neck, holding him tight. Her mouth opened, her soft lips parting in welcome, her cold, chocolaty tongue plunging against his.

When they finally drew apart for breath, he said, "I can tell something's wrong and you've had a shitty day. What will make you feel better—talking about it, or getting made love to until you can't even remember your own name, much less what was wrong?"

She gazed up at him, a tiny hint of a smile appearing on those beautiful lips. Instead of answering, she grabbed a fistful of his shirt, turned and pulled him toward her bedroom.

Oh, good. Hot sex instead of conversation. That would have been his first choice, too.

He followed her for a couple of steps, then stopped, bent and swept her up into his arms. Any woman who'd had a day as bad as hers deserved to be swept off her feet by a man who was crazy about her.

And he was crazy about her. Head-over-heels, out-of-his-mind, now-and-forever mad about her.

He had fallen into lust at first sight the night they met. Now, his emotions were fully engaged by this woman. Hers was the face he pictured when he drifted off to sleep every night, and the first thing he thought of every morning. He'd already fallen into an I-have-to-tell-Mimi-about-this habit, so used to having her in his life already, even though he hadn't even known her a couple of weeks ago.

His father had once told him he'd fallen in love with his mother, who he barely knew, when he saw her angrily confront a man who had made a racist remark to a passing stranger.

Xander had fallen when he'd seen Mimi up in that tree, trying to rescue that dumb cat.

In her room, he dropped her onto the bed. She immediately reached up to pull her blouse free of her pants, but he put his hands on hers, stopping her.

"Just lie there and let me take care of you."

"But..."

"Let me," he insisted.

She did as he asked, letting her hand fall to her side, any further protests dying on her lips. She watched wide-eyed as he pulled his own shirt up and off. Sitting on the edge of the bed, he kicked off his boots but kept his pants on. This wasn't about him getting naked, it was about getting her relaxed. Giving her something else to think about—something to feel good about.

He began to slowly unbutton her silky blouse, taking his time, letting her know he had the patience to do things right. When his knuckles scraped across the curve of her breast, she moaned a little, but she didn't twist closer or demand he speed things up.

Once she was all unbuttoned, he spread the blouse open, then sat back on his heels to look at the pretty, pale pink bra she wore underneath. It wasn't as pretty as her skin, not nearly as pretty as the puckered nipples he could see beneath the lace, but it was damned nice nonetheless.

The bra clasped in the front, and he reached down and flicked it open with his thumb. The two sides pulled apart, freeing her lush breasts. He bent to one, kissing her again and again, all over the vulnerable flesh. Then he moved to the other, sampling her, drawing things out, building them up.

"Xander," she groaned, reaching up and tangling her fingers in his hair.

He couldn't resist the desperate plea in her voice, and finally moved his mouth over one puckered nipple. She arched up toward him, offering him more of her breast, and he sucked her gently, deliberately.

Her pleased cries were music in his ears. This wasn't demanding, wasn't frenzied. He wanted her boneless, breathless, without thought or worry. And he was willing to take all night to get her that way.

But he didn't imagine it would take that long.

After devoting serious attention to both her breasts, he resumed his slow undressing, moving to her waistband and unbuttoning her pants. She lifted up to help him pull them off.

"There's my favorite view in the world," he said as he peeled off her skimpy panties to reveal the lovely, womanly place between her legs.

"You've certainly seen enough of it to judge," she told him with a throaty chuckle.

"You're just so beautiful," he said, stroking her upper thigh, her hip, the indentation just above her pubic bone.

So beautiful. So responsive.

She was panting now, her hips thrusting up in tiny undulations as he toyed with her gingery curls. When he slipped his hand down to the folds of her sex, he found her warm and slippery, totally aroused.

"Please," she whispered.

He gave her a little taste of the penetration he knew she needed, sliding his finger into her tight channel. She clenched around him, whimpering, and he gave her another finger, slowly making love to her with both.

Filling her was good—very good. But he wanted to bring her to even higher heights. So he stroked her carefully until he found that soft, spongy spot way up inside her and toyed with it, bringing a sharp gasp to her lips.

"Okay?"

"Do that again," she ordered.

He did, this time dropping his thumb onto her clit, pleasuring both her pleasure points at the same time.

"Oh, yes," she groaned.

He kept up the strokes, taking cues from her cries, letting her set the pace. She did, slow at first, then speeding up as her climax built. When it finally washed over her—sending a flush through her entire body and making her cry out—he moved away long enough to strip out of his clothes.

He was back between her parted thighs before she'd stopped moaning. And was sliding his aching cock into her before she'd even begun to fall back to earth.

"Oh, Xander," she whispered, wrapping her arms around his shoulders and her legs around his hips, "you definitely know how to make a bad day into a good one."

"Protect and serve, that's my motto," he said, gently thrusting into her again.

"I thought that was for cops."

"Whatever."

Then he couldn't speak, couldn't laugh, he could only feel. He was inside the body of the woman he was falling in love with, wrapped within her embrace, held as intimately as a man could be held, and didn't want his own thoughts to interfere with the moment. He just went with it—went with the pleasure and the rightness of it.

They rocked together, slower, more gently than they'd ever gone before, exchanging long kisses and tender caresses. And, he knew, doing something more.

They'd had wild, crazy sex all week. This time, they were making love, exchanging vows and promises without ever saying a word.

He'd never felt so moved. Never been so sure of anything in his life as he was of this moment and this place and this woman.

She gasped, her eyelashes fluttering as a climax rolled over her again, brought about by the slow grind of their bodies. Xander had been drawing things out, content to wait, loving the trip and not needing to arrive at the destination. But when he felt the tight clenching of her body, it wrung the last bit of resistance right out of him. He followed her, her utter satisfaction triggering his own release.

Knowing he was about to come, Xander cupped her face in his hands, staring into her eyes, and said, "Say something so I'll know this isn't a dream. It feels too perfect to be real."

She smiled, holding him even tighter as he spilled into her.

"If it's a dream, I hope neither of us ever wakes up."

10

MIMI'S MOOD HAD DEFINITELY lifted during their amazing, powerful love-making. But afterward, she couldn't prevent that mix of sadness, rage and disappointment she'd been feeling much of the day from creeping back in and affecting her mood.

While Xander showered, she went into the kitchen and got out some stuff to make them some dinner, going over everything in her mind one more time. By the time she'd gotten to the point of making salad, she was angry enough again that she was hacking at a head of lettuce with a butcher knife.

"Whoa, there," he said as he entered the kitchen, toweling off his hair. She lost herself for a moment, gazing at those flexing muscles of his arms. God, she would never tire of looking at this man.

"I don't think that's the iceberg that sunk the *Titanic,*" he added.

She got the joke but couldn't manage much more than a tiny smile.

Xander went to the fridge and helped himself to a

beer, then turned and leaned a hip against the counter, watching her work. "Are you ready to talk about it?"

She was, having felt like she was going to explode most of the day with the need to vent. She'd only been able to say so much to Lauren, since Mimi's father was her boss, too, but with Xander there were no such restrictions.

So she told him, launching into a full description of what had happened that morning in her office. When she mentioned the it's-your-fault part of the conversation, she saw Xander's jaw start to clench. And when she got to the I'd-fire-you, he crossed his flexing arms over his broad chest and thrust his fisted hands under them, as if to hide the fact that they were shaking with anger.

"You're too good at your job to let something like that happen," he said, his indignation a living thing in the tiny kitchen.

"Thank you," she murmured, her ramrod-straight posture easing a bit. His belief in her went a long way toward calming her down.

"Did Dimitri even try to come to your defense?"

She grunted.

"Douchebag."

"He upset me, but honestly, the longer the day went on, the less I cared about his reaction and the more my father's hurt."

He walked over and put a hand on her shoulder. "He was having a bad day and lashed out. He may be guilty of bad managerial skills, but you know he loves you."

She covered his hand with hers and squeezed. "I know."

Waiting for the lettuce to dry before she could finish the salad, she went back to the fridge to get the marinated chicken they planned to throw onto the grill.

"So what happened at the meeting?"

"First, I have to back up to the hour before the meeting. It was crazy."

She'd been opening her mouth to yell for Lauren the minute the two men had left that morning. But she hadn't even needed to. Her assistant had been in her office—with the initialed ad proofs—before Mimi could make a sound.

"Listening at keyholes?" she'd asked the younger woman, not angry, just relieved she was so on the ball.

"Of course. Isn't that what you pay me for?" Lauren had replied before spreading out the proofs on her desk.

She told Xander that, and about how they'd gone over everything inch by inch, confirming there had been no random penises in the Burdette Quality Foods circular.

Mimi had then gone on to examine all the communication between her staff and the printer. Lauren was smart enough to always send cybercorrespondence with a receipt request, so she could prove exactly which digital file the other company had received and when they had received it.

Armed with all the proof, Mimi had gotten on the phone with the printer. And by the time the one hour between the sneak attack in her office and the scheduled meeting had elapsed, she'd had the initially blustering printer in tears on the phone. He'd been unable to deny the evidence, and swore he'd find out who had sabotaged the ad immediately.

She was walking into the meeting with her father, alone, not needing any staff when she had evidence, when Lauren had dashed up and whispered that the printer had already called. His cartoon-drawing grandson, who worked for him, had confessed. Case closed.

An hour and some good investigative work had been enough to clear her name. She didn't know how long it would take to get over the fact that her own father hadn't given her the same benefit of the doubt he would give any other employee.

After she had relayed the story to Xander, he nodded, but didn't smile and try to say everything was all right. He knew better. They'd talked enough about her job, her mixed feelings about it, her struggles with her father, for him to know this had been a blow from which it would be hard to recover.

"So what are you going to do now?" Xander asked, proving he realized that even though the mystery had been solved, and she had been absolved of all responsibility—and had received an apology from her father and Dimitri—she hadn't finished dealing with it.

"Honestly, I don't know," she admitted. "I can't just let it go. As much as I hate to fight with Dad, I'm going to have to let him know how I feel. I'll never respect myself again if I let the fact that I want to be CEO stop me from standing up for myself when I've been treated so badly."

"You're right, you won't." He frowned, as if he wanted to say more, but hesitated.

"What?"

"I was just wondering if you've ever thought about working anywhere else."

She nodded slowly. "Believe it or not, I've thought about it more than once lately." She rubbed her hands up and down her arms, though it wasn't really chilly. "I don't hate my job. I've always liked the idea of trying to bring it into the twenty-first century. It's my family legacy, mine by *right.* But I don't know… Would I choose it if my grandfather hadn't founded it? I just don't know."

He obviously heard her vehemence. "Right. And maybe your relationship with your father would be a little better if the boss/employee strain were lifted."

"Maybe. But should I give up my career goals when I know, deep down, we would both be hurt by that? Because even if he is a sexist jerk, in the long run, I know he realizes I'd be damn good and would be the right hands in which to entrust his father's business."

Xander sipped his beer, nodding, looking like he was considering it but not totally convinced.

"You have to understand how badly I wanted this growing up," she insisted. "The fact that I was born a girl, and some people thought I shouldn't be entitled to it, only made me that much more determined to prove everyone wrong. To not only get the job, but also to be the best CEO we've ever had."

"You could," he said softly.

She warmed at the compliment, knowing he had not one iota of firsthand knowledge of what she was like at work, and was basing his assessment totally on his faith in her. Something few people had ever done for her in her life.

"I have a million plans," she said. Plans that she'd never revealed to anyone. "Our expansion into the northeast, adding a farmer's market and dining areas, becoming more of a center for the community in small towns that don't have many social outlets."

"Sounds great."

It did. And she could make it happen.

But not if she was always treated like the daughter-who-would-someday-screw-up. She already had to work harder than any other executive on staff, and got half the credit and twice as much blame. She didn't know what else she had to do to prove her point. Screwups like today sure weren't going to help.

"Do you think your father would ever let you do any of it?"

And there was the rub. Because the truth was, no, she didn't. So if she wanted to make those ideas become reality, she'd have to wait until he retired and she took over. Which could take another decade. Could she really stand another decade like this?

"I don't know," she admitted. "Maybe if I left, proved myself elsewhere, and then came back in a few years."

"Maybe," he insisted, putting down his beer and walking over to take her in his arms. "Just keep all the possibilities in the back of your mind, would you? There's not much you couldn't do if you set your mind to it, Mimi."

She lifted her eyes to study his handsome, serious face, seeing his sincerity. Seeing his absolute, unwavering faith in her.

What an amazing, remarkable gift she'd been given, so suddenly, so unexpectedly. He had come out of nowhere—or, at least, her closet—and was already the best thing that had ever happened to her.

"I will," she said with a smile, so warmed by his reassurance that she could barely remember how badly she'd felt earlier today. "Now, ready to go out back? I hear voices and suspect the grill's already been fired up."

"We never did have that community barbecue to welcome Helen and her kid."

"No, we didn't."

Mimi had seen the other woman and the little boy a few times this week, actually sitting down and having a glass of sweet tea with Helen on the back porch one night when Xander had to work. She liked Anna and Obi-Wan's daughter. A lot. And she couldn't help wondering if, now that Helen appeared to be "over" her traumatic divorce, perhaps she might be looking at reheating things with Dimitri. His name had come up only briefly. Neither woman had asked, or answered, any personal questions, though Helen—well, everyone in the house—knew Mimi and Xander were already involved. So she had to wonder if Helen had been thinking along those lines.

As for what Dimitri thought about his ex having moved to Athens, she didn't know. They hadn't had a personal conversation since he'd left her place last weekend, and she wasn't feeling very charitably toward him right now so she doubted they would anytime soon.

"Let's go," she said, pushing the big bowl of salad into his hands.

Since they had containers of food and drink, they didn't go through the closet, but rather left her apartment and went out through the community part of the house. When they exited the back door, they nearly bumped into Helen, who stood nearby, her hands clenched together in front of her. Her son stood at her side, and his mouth was hanging open and his eyes almost comically wide.

Mimi immediately turned and looked in the same direction, toward the garage. Anna stood there. Judging by her frown, the arms crossed over her chest, and the impatiently tapping foot, she wasn't happy.

A few feet away stood Obi-Wan, whose jaw was stuck out in a belligerent pose. He was holding a plastic baseball bat, which she'd last seen in Tuck's hands. He appeared to be trying to get around Anna, who was blocking him with her body, and ordering him to stop being such a fool.

Shifting her gaze again, she realized what Anna was trying to keep Obi-Wan from reaching. Or, rather *who* she was trying to keep him from reaching.

A short guy wearing an old-fashioned suit stood behind Anna, trying to hide or disappear. That wasn't the strange part, though.

The donkey head he was wearing was what took the situation from the typically unusual kind of thing that went on around here to a whole new level of bizarro.

"I said, put that thing away," Anna snapped. "You're being ridiculous."

"You can't parade your boyfriend around in my own backyard and expect me not to do anything about it," Obi-Wan said, swinging the plastic bat menacingly. It was about the most passionate she'd ever seen the man, whose Zen attitude usually rivaled Buddha's. "I'll bop you right between those long ears if you don't stay away from my wife, you no-talent ham!"

Ahh. This was the actor, the one Anna was supposedly having the affair with. He wasn't much to look at. At least, not from the neck down, being scrawny and pale, with liver-spotted hands that shook as he grabbed Anna's shoulders and used her as a human shield.

She glared at him over her shoulder and shook the hands off, obviously none too pleased with him, either. "You knock it off or I'll let him get you. I can't believe you spread those awful lies about me—about us!"

There came a muffled jumble of words in response.

"Oh, take that ridiculous thing off," Anna said, skewering him with a look. "I don't care about your method acting or that tonight's the final dress rehearsal. You look like a ninny."

Then she turned back to her husband. "I owe you an apology."

Obi-Wan lowered the bat, but instead of looking relieved, an expression of sheer horror filled his face. "You mean…it's true? You're admitting it?"

Anna walked closer, putting her hand on her husband's chest. "No, it's absolutely not true. But I had no idea about these rumors that were going around—" she jerked her thumb over her shoulder, gesturing toward the ass-head "—courtesy of him. I thought you were just being paranoid. Then I heard him saying some awful lies."

Obi-Wan lifted the bat and tried to get around her again. "Let me at him."

"No, no, it's all right," she insisted, "he's nothing to worry about, nothing but a Boba Fett."

A brief pause, then they both laughed together. Xander gave Mimi a curious look, but she didn't take time to explain. Obi-Wan and Anna had their own language, and she'd once told Mimi that Obi-Wan considered that particular *Star Wars* character an ignoble, dishonorable villain, not even worthy of using a lightsaber on. Unlike Darth Vader. Or something like that.

"And you might break Tuck's bat, or damage the costume, which I'll end up having to repair."

The actor, who had struggled to get the full-head mask off without assistance, stared bug-eyed at the married couple. They'd been fighting a moment before, but now looked about to melt into each other's arms.

Frankly, Mimi thought the "other man" looked better as a donkey.

"I'm sorry," he stammered, "I just got carried away with my role."

"Well, you've played the role of horse's ass all your life, Fred," said Obi-Wan. "So this shouldn't have been that much of a stretch!"

The nervous little man stammered more apologies, then slipped out of the yard practically unnoticed. Anna and Obi-Wan suddenly had eyes only for each other. They were going back into one of their madly-in-love phases, which were among the happiest times to live in this house. Because when they were "on," there was no couple more romantic or more wildly in love. As if even the fireflies of the woods surrounding the house had gotten the news, they all suddenly started to illuminate, setting the early evening a-twinkle. Love just seemed to have the power to light the world.

Mimi wondered if the owners of the house might soon have a little competition in the most-romantic/most-in-love department. Because she and Xander's romance hadn't exactly been storybook perfect, but oh, was it ever wonderful.

And she *was* falling in love with him. Madly, crazily. Completely. She'd never felt anything like this in her life, had no other definition or explanation, and knew he'd captured her mind, body and soul. No man had ever come close to making her feel the things she felt when she was with him, physically and emotionally.

It would probably be a while before she would be ready to reveal that to him, considering their relationship was still so new, so fragile. But someday she would, and she hoped he'd be as glad to hear the words as she would be to say them.

"So Grandpa's not gonna beat up the horse-man?"

"Definitely not," said Helen, ruffling her little boy's hair. She then glanced toward Xander and Mimi. "Welcome. Join the insanity."

Mimi laughed. "Hey, you're the one who decided to move back here."

Her tender smile as she eyed her parents, now kissing in the sunset, told Mimi that Helen didn't regret that decision one bit.

With Obi-Wan and Anna now back together, the evening took on even more of a celebratory tone. Will, the quiet writer from the second floor, came down with his famous homemade sangria, Anna had whipped up her special potato salad and everyone shared food and laughter as the sun set.

As strange as it seemed, to Mimi, this felt more like a family dinner than any of the Sunday-afternoon gatherings she spent at her parents' estate. Because, as much as she cared about her mother, father and extended family, she was never entirely sure the *real* Mimi was present at those types of events, or if she was just the Mimi she was expected to be.

Here, she didn't even have to give it a second thought. She could say what she thought and mean what she said. Could let out an unladylike snort when she laughed. Could eat a hot dog without a lifted brow and a reminder of calorie count from her anorexic aunt. Could laugh with all the others when Anna reminded everyone of the time Mimi had run out of dishwasher detergent and used the regular liquid soap in her machine, causing bubbles to slowly spread throughout most of the downstairs before anybody had noticed. She could be a bit of a klutz and laugh at herself, rather than stressing so hard to be careful and cautious that she ended up dropping and breaking something she'd been anxious to keep from harm.

And she could do it all with Xander's hand curled in hers, or his arm across her shoulders.

That was one of the hardest things of all to picture—bringing Xander around her family. Not that she was worried about how her family would react to him, but rather how he would react to them!

He had told her enough about his upbringing that she knew he had strong family values. He was happy with his middle-class idea of the good life, and had a total faith in the equality of all, no matter their race, sex or bank account.

Xander had been shocked by her father's sexist attitude toward her. She shuddered, not even wanting to imagine what he'd say if he ever realized her parents actually still had those horrid, racist lawn-jockey statues on either side of the driveway leading to their house. Mimi cringed whenever she saw them, had begged her folks to get rid of them, and had even intentionally knocked them over with her car on more than one occasion. But there they remained, what her parents saw as quaint and she considered horribly offensive.

She'd hate for Xander to think she shared those attitudes. And even though she didn't, there were times when she found herself having to fulfill the role in which she'd been cast in other ways. She had to wear the clothes and the jewelry, socialize with those people, move in that circle.

What would happen if he ever saw the Mimi she had to be when she was in that world? Would he know it wasn't the real her? Would he still want her? Would he still even like her?

She was dwelling on that a little too much, letting it interfere with her evening, so she forced the thoughts out of her head. By eight o'clock she'd laughed away most of the dark reminders of the day, and the last thing she wanted was to go back to the dour mental place she'd been in when she'd gotten home from work.

But suddenly, something happened that made her realize she might not be that lucky. Because the side gate was swinging inward. And two familiar heads were walking through it, about to crash the happy party.

Her father. And Dimitri.

"Oh, hell," she snapped, her heart sinking and all the delicious food she'd just consumed churning in her stomach.

"What's wrong?" Xander asked. He turned around

to see what had caught her attention, and his hand tightened on her knee. "It's okay. I'll bet you ten bucks they're here to apologize."

"I just wanted one evening when I didn't have to deal with it," she muttered.

"I know. But I'm here." He gestured to the others around the table, who'd also fallen silent, watching the new arrivals walk across the lawn. "We're all here for you."

Mimi nodded her thanks, then slowly rose from her seat. She cast a quick glance at Helen, wondering how she was taking Dimitri's arrival, and noticed the pretty brunette seemed fine. She hadn't been caught off-guard this time, like she had on Saturday. Helen seemed to have her calm-and-collected mask in place, ready to deal with a man she still very obviously had feelings for.

Forcing herself to relax, Mimi walked to her father and pressed a kiss on his cheek. Then she nodded at Dimitri. "This is a surprise."

"Honey," said her dad, "I just couldn't wait until tomorrow to make sure you understand how sorry I am about how I acted this morning. Knowing Dimitri felt the same way, I got him to bring me over here to see you."

Dimitri nodded in confirmation. "I'm terribly sorry, too, Mimi."

She managed a tight smile. "Thanks. But you've both already said that. You didn't need to come out here and say it again."

"Well, it wasn't just an apology we came out here to offer," said Dad. "We've been at the office, talking about the whole thing, about you, how well you handled it. We couldn't be prouder."

Yippie. But not. Because, again, hurt twisted in her gut.

It was the "we" that got to her. Her father could have done this on his own. Instead, he'd felt the need to include Dimitri, who'd been a stranger to them all of six months ago.

If it had been a boss apologizing, and they'd done it at work, it would have been different. But they'd come here to her home, which made it personal. And personally speaking, she was sick of feeling like she, herself, was never quite good enough for her father to bother with on his own.

Her father couldn't have made it much more clear that he was disappointed to have never had a son, only a daughter. But would it have killed him to, just once in a while, make the effort to pretend he was okay with it?

"Maybe we should go inside," she said. "Talk in private."

Dad gestured toward the others at the table. "Nonsense, we're among your friends, aren't we?" He managed to not convey the frank shock he usually expressed that she enjoyed socializing with her neighbors…or that she lived here at all. "Besides, I'm sure you'll want to share your good news with them."

"Good news?" she asked, her brow furrowing in confusion.

"Of course." He came closer, dropping his hands onto her shoulders. "You proved something to me today. You proved you're a lot more than a pretty face with my last name."

She gasped.

That's a compliment, he's trying to offer you a compliment.

Repeating that mantra in her head didn't stop her from feeling like she'd just been kicked in the nuts. If she had nuts. Which she didn't, of course. But she had to imagine it was at least as painful as hearing your own father say something so shitty.

At the table, she saw Xander rise to his feet, a dark frown on his face. He'd obviously heard, and looked ready to walk over and give her some backup. Not wanting to go into that whole conversation yet, she deterred him with a tiny shake of her head.

"Thanks," she managed to choke out.

Still not even realizing how badly he'd hurt and insulted her, her clueless father continued. "You've shown me that you've got the stuff to go higher. You're getting a promotion."

This time, her gasp wasn't caused by pain but by genuine surprise. "Really?"

"Yes. I've been thinking about my retirement in a few years."

Her heart raced. Was this finally going to happen? Had he really changed his mind about giving her his job when he retired? After all this effort, all the sixty-hour work weeks, the stressful meetings, the long business trips, had it really just taken a cartoon penis to give her what she'd always wanted?

Her dad dropped an arm across her shoulders, and stepped closer to Dimitri so the three of them stood within a small circle. "And with Dimitri there to always advise and guide you, I think I can allow the two of you to run the company when I'm gone. Together. As man and wife."

THOUGH MR. BURDETTE had lowered his voice a little, everyone at the table heard the last bit of the conversation taking place across the lawn. Including Xander, who immediately coughed into his fist when Mimi's father made a couple of huge assumptions about his daughter.

First, that she'd need anybody's help or guidance to run the company in which she'd already invested all of her adult life.

Second, that it would be Dimitri she'd need that help from.

And third—big, huge, ridiculous assumption—that she'd marry the dude in order to get the job she already damn well deserved.

This time, he couldn't stop himself from jumping in. He strode over to Mimi and the idiots on either side of her, snapping, "That's nuts."

Mimi, whose mouth was still hanging open in shock, as if she couldn't even find any words, eyed him gratefully.

"Excuse me, who, exactly, are you?" Burdette asked, one brow going up in a supercilious expression.

"I'm Xander McKinley," he said. "Your daughter's… friend."

Her father might not have understood the pause, but the ex-boyfriend sure did. Dimitri's whole body jerked, his back going so straight he could have been set down at the edge of a pool and used as a diving board. He couldn't have looked more shocked if he'd opened the

Wall Street Journal and found out his portfolio bubble had suddenly burst.

Well, maybe one bubble had. His I'm-irreplaceable bubble.

"Well, as my daughter's friend, I would think you'd be congratulating her about now," her father said, looking back and forth between Mimi and the two men. This time, he didn't sound arrogant, but rather genuinely confused. "She's getting the job she's always wanted, and a marriage proposal…." He suddenly broke off, flushing lightly. "I apologize, Dimitri, I realize we hadn't talked about that part on the way over. Perhaps we should have taken Mimi's suggestion and gone inside so you could ask her properly."

We should have gone inside. Meaning the proud papa would have been standing right there to give his blessing over what should be a very private moment between two people.

Of course, that moment wasn't gonna happen. No way, no how. Not between those two people, anyway.

To give him credit, Dimitri now looked as lost for words as Mimi. His throat wobbled as he swallowed. And, for some reason, instead of glancing at the woman he was being ordered to propose to, he cast a quick, anxious stare toward the table. Toward Helen.

Xander watched as she stared back, the color draining out of her pretty face. When she mumbled an excuse about needing to go inside for something and dashed into the house, Dimitri took the tiniest step, as if to go after her. But that's as far as he got. Whether he was held back by his feelings for Mimi, his concerns about his job or just gutlessness, Xander couldn't say.

Mimi finally found her voice. "Dad, this is madness. I'm not going to marry Dimitri."

"Of course you are, it's all arranged!"

Dimitri cleared his throat. "Now look, Philip, I know you said you wanted…"

"They're not even dating anymore," Xander snapped, unable to stay out of the conversation. Something inside him rebelled at the very mention of Mimi being with anybody except himself. "She dumped him last weekend. They're finished, and she's moved on."

All three of them turned their focus directly on him. Except, Mimi's didn't stay there. She dropped her lashes quickly, hiding her eyes. And Xander started to feel an unpleasant tingling in the base of his spine.

"You did break up with him, right?" he asked her, needing her to confirm it.

"No, she didn't," Dimitri said.

Xander froze, so shocked he didn't know *what* to say.

Mimi had lied to him? She was still with this dude, who might want to propose to her, but might also want to run in after his ex? And both of them were dancing on the ends of the puppet strings being jerked by a Southern millionaire who had obviously been reincarnated from an age when fathers did shit like arrange their adult daughters' marriages to men who would "advise and guide" them.

Crazy. It was all entirely, completely crazy.

But craziest of all was that first, initial fact that had slammed him hard in the heart: Mimi had lied to him. She'd been sleeping with him all week, sharing the most amazingly intimate moments, sharing conversations and dreams and fantasies. And all the while, she'd been stringing along another—more suitable—guy. The one her father had obviously handpicked for her.

The one she had to marry if she wanted the job of her dreams.

"I'm sorry," Xander said, his tone as icy as his heart suddenly felt. "I was obviously misinformed."

"There was nothing to break up," Mimi insisted, her attention totally on him. "We weren't even…"

"What is going *on* here?" Philip Burdette interrupted, finally cluing in to the vibe swirling around the rest of them. Then he threw a hand up, palm out. "Never mind, I don't want to know. I'll only say this—Mimi, you've always said you wanted what's best for our family, to continue our proud heritage, and I've believed you. If you meant it, you'll do the right thing. Marry Dimitri, run the company with him, preserve it for your children and your children's children."

"Dad, I'm not going to…"

"*Marry him* and run it together, or forget about ever taking over as CEO."

She jerked as if she'd been slapped.

Xander was mad as hell at Mimi, feeling betrayed and gutted, but his heart was also breaking for her. Thinking of the moments he'd had with his own parents, the way they'd never, in his entire lifetime, made him feel anything less than loved, appreciated and wanted, he longed to take her in his arms and soothe her.

But he couldn't. Not now, not when he was still angry. Not now when he really had no idea where he stood with the woman.

One thing he could do was say his piece to Mr. Rich-

and-Arrogant, who obviously got his way a little too often and hadn't learned to take no for an answer.

"She doesn't love him," he snapped. "And if you don't change your ways, and your attitude, pretty soon she's not going to love you, either."

Burdette flinched, then began to sputter.

Xander ignored him. "Don't you realize what you've done, and what you're on the verge of throwing away? If I ever had a daughter and made her feel *half* as crappy about herself as you do, or ever gave one tiny hint that I wasn't overjoyed to have been blessed with my child's presence in my life—no matter what their sex—I'd go right out and jump off a bridge."

He was breathing hard, feeling the heat in his face, and glowering at the older man, so it took a second before he heard the clapping. Casting a quick glance across the lawn, he saw Anna, Obi-Wan and Will all applauding and nodding their agreement.

As for Burdette, he was so red in the face he looked like his head was about to pop of. His mouth kept jerking, and his head shaking, like he was forming an entire litany of scathing retorts, but couldn't come up with just the right one to lead off the assault.

Mimi was watching in silence, tears streaming down her face. Dimitri had grown a little pale, and had shoved his hands in his pockets.

And Xander had just had enough.

Christ, these people didn't know the meaning of sacrifice or loss or heartache. Perfect jobs and getting to push people around and always dancing to somebody else's tune...what a lot of bullshit. None of it mattered a damn compared to love and loss, to family and commitment.

He wondered if any of them would even understand the concept if he tried to explain it.

Doubtful. Right now, he wasn't even sure Mimi got it, and that broke his heart more than anything.

So without as much as another glance at any of them, he turned on his heel.

"Xander!" Mimi called.

It was damned hard, but he managed to ignore her. He couldn't talk to her, not right now, not until he had calmed down and really thought about whether he wanted someone to have the power to hurt him the way she just had.

So, without a single backward glance, he strode out of the yard to his car, got in it and drove away as fast and as far as he could.

11

BY THE TIME MIMI had gotten her brain functioning again and realized Xander was leaving, it had been too late to stop him. Nor had she had the slightest clue where he might have gone. So instead of going after him, which she desperately wanted to do, she'd stayed put and cleared the air, once and for-all, with her father.

It had been bad.

It had also been incredibly liberating.

She'd felt positively released, finally being able to say what she thought and felt. Xander's parting words had filled her with confidence, because he'd verbalized everything she'd always felt but hadn't been able to say.

She only wished he'd stayed around to hear it.

"Where are you?" she mumbled, glancing at the clock and seeing it was after one.

She'd tried calling his cell phone and had left a few messages. Had tried the station house. Eventually, she had accepted the fact that he would come back when he was ready to talk and she just had to deal with the wait. It was the least she could do, considering what he'd done for her.

No one had ever stood up for her like that. The way he had taken her side, leaping to her defense, even when he was angry with her, had brought tears to her eyes.

And steel to her spine.

It was the echo of Xander's words that she'd heard when she'd finally given her father an answer to his ridiculous ultimatum. And his strength she'd borrowed from to stand firm against the hurricane that had broken over her head when she'd done it. Thankfully, the storm hadn't included any squalls from Dimitri, who'd quietly insisted he had no intention of proposing, thank God. Of course, after that, her father had then been furious with them both.

I need to thank you, Xander. I need to hold you.

I need to tell you I love you.

But she couldn't do a damn thing until he came home.

So she went to bed, thinking about tomorrow, about the conversation they'd have. About how she had to make him believe her when she told him everything that was in her heart and all the wishes and dreams that filled her soul.

They'd have a lot of time to talk, no doubt about that.

Oy. Unemployment wasn't going to be fun. But instead of making her worry, the thought actually made her grin.

Quitting her job might have been impulsive and emotional and scary as hell. But now that she'd done it, she had realized it was the only way she could ever be happy. Not only because she needed to go out and prove herself, but also because she would never have a decent relationship with her family until she separated her business life from her private one.

Her father would forgive her. Someday. Hopefully.

Finally, when the clock was nearing three and she still felt no nearer to relaxing, she got up and went into the kitchen. She was about to pour herself a glass of milk when she spotted the little pouch of tea that Obi-Wan had given her a couple of weeks ago. There was enough left for one more cup. She hadn't touched it again after that second night, and now felt in the need of a few soothing, relaxing sips. Maybe it would help her get a few hours' sleep before what she thought could be the most important conversation of her life.

Brewing the cup and carrying it to her room, she took a small sip. And once again, like the last time, all her senses awakened and her memories began to churn, taunting her with images she couldn't quite place. It was as if a stream of warm lava had been inserted into her body, sending sensation rushing through her.

She relaxed in the bed. And just as she was falling asleep, remembered the wild, erotic dream she'd had the second time she'd consumed some of Obi-Wan's tea. It had been wicked—there had been two men, hadn't there? Two men at first, anyway, but by the end of the dream, there had only been one. The right one. Below her, behind her, on top of her, whispering in her ear, kissing her neck, making beautiful love to her.

Only one.

The only one she ever needed. Xander.

With that thought in mind, she let her eyes drop

closed, hoping she'd have a dream just as lovely. Especially if she could awaken to winning Xander's heart in reality.

SHE WAS IN A CASTLE.

She didn't know whose castle, or where it was, or even if she belonged there. She only knew she felt trapped. Suffocated.

Pacing back and forth in a small room, she measured passing time by the tap of her feet against the stone floor and the matching beats of her heart. She realized her room was in a tall tower, because she could look out the window and see the forest far down below. And beyond it was a cliff and that rocky ocean over which she sometimes liked to fly.

Fly? She couldn't fly. What a silly thought. Everybody always told her she couldn't fly.

But somebody had once showed her she could, hadn't they? And she wanted to, so very badly. She wanted to climb through that small window and throw herself out, not to fall to the ground below, but to soar even higher above it. To be free of these walls and the weight of something heavy, tugging at her shoulders.

She thought she could. Felt sure she could.

She began to climb.

A knock sounded at the door. "It's time," a man called. He knocked again, then again, insistently, each rap of knuckle on wood a jab at her soul.

"Time for what?"

"Don't be silly, time for the ceremony."

Ceremony? She blinked, shook her head, trying to remember.

"Come on, you can't be late!"

The door opened and a man appeared, beckoning her out. He was older, gray-haired, and wore the plush, purple-velvet robes and crown of a king.

"Your Majesty," she said, awed and a little overwhelmed.

He looked her over from head to toe. "It's not perfect, but it's all right."

She looked down and realized she was wearing the most beautiful, exquisite bridal gown she had ever seen. Mimi looked like a fairy princess, an angel, a Victoria's Secret model only not mostly naked. How could this man say it wasn't perfect?

But, in one way, she realized, he was right. The dress was so very heavy—adorned with beads and jewels. It's what pulled on her shoulders, making each step a chore, tugging her down, keeping her earthbound.

"Why am I dressed like this?"

"Just be quiet and do what I say. I know best. It'll be fine," he said. "Now hurry and put on your shoes, I'll be outside."

He left and she was alone.

She looked at the shoes, lifted her hand to reach for them, but then let it fall.

"I don't want to wear the shoes. I don't want to wear this dress. It weighs so much and doesn't suit me."

"Then don't," a voice whispered.

Startled, she looked around the room but saw no one. The stone walls were solid—no person could be hiding in the chamber.

"Over here," he said.

She glanced toward the window, and there he was.

Her black-draped, shadowy stranger. He was standing on the ledge, as if he'd just landed there, mysterious and unknowable. Again, that mist covered his face and she couldn't see him clearly, but she recognized the strong arms, the broad chest, the powerful, massive body.

She walked over, her pulse racing, excitement making her shake.

He reached for her hand. She gave it to him, not hesitating, and allowed him to pull her up to join him on the ledge. They were so high, so very high, and the ledge was so small. But she felt no fear.

"Are we going to fly again?"

He shook his head and disappointment washed over her.

"You don't have to fly," he said. He ran a black-gloved finger down her cheek and the touch soothed and thrilled her, all at the same time. "You can walk out of here anytime you want."

She looked down and saw that he was right. The ground was no longer far below, it was directly beneath her window. All she had to do as step down and walk away.

She glanced toward the door, knowing the king was waiting on the other side of it. Then she focused on the stranger, who had moved closer, so that his beautiful mouth could brush against her temple. "I'll be waiting," he said. "Come find me once you get out."

He hopped down onto the soft carpet of pale green grass below. Lifting his hand, he offered her a flower. A magnolia. The most lovely, perfect one she had ever seen. It was huge, creamy white, and the sweet fragrance filled her every breath with heady delight.

"For you," he said.

Just before he left, the mist cleared. She saw his face clearly for the first time.

She knew that face. She knew the twinkling brown eyes. She knew the strong jaw, the full mouth, the high brow.

She knew him. And she loved him.

Mimi opened her mouth to tell him that.

But he was already gone.

XANDER HADN'T DONE a whole lot of exploring when he'd moved to Georgia. He'd had to start his job right away and his days off had been taken up with finding a place to live, then actually moving into it. And, of course, Mimi.

But with time on his hands, some anger to drive off, and no particular destination in mind, he'd found himself exploring the state. He'd driven across flat farmland and down long, windy roads and small towns with ramshackle houses.

Every mile he traveled took him farther away from Athens.

But every mile he traveled also brought him closer to Mimi.

Because as much as he tried to hold on to his righteous anger, eventually he had finally had to admit the truth—she hadn't lied to him. Technically speaking, he hadn't asked her if she'd broken up with Dimitri, he'd asked her if they were over. She'd said yes, and, in her heart, mind and soul, she had meant it.

Over the days that had followed, there might have been times when she should have realized what he'd assumed. But maybe she hadn't. Maybe, as she'd said to him before, there had really been nothing to get "over" since she and Dimitri had never been a real couple to begin with.

He didn't know. He only knew she deserved the chance to explain, and he had the right to ask.

It was dawn when he got back to the old plantation house, which had become home so quickly, he almost couldn't remember what his apartment building in Chicago had looked like. Maybe that was because of her, too. Probably it was.

Inside, he didn't go to his door, but, instead, to hers. He used the key she'd given him, let himself in and headed for her bedroom. The lights were off, all was quiet, and for the tiniest second, an evil, doubtful voice tried to warn him to be prepared to find just about anything in her room. Like her with her fiancé.

No. Not a chance.

She wouldn't do it in a million years. Not his Mimi. Not the woman he'd come to know and love. In fact, he would probably find her wide-awake, wondering if he was okay, worried more about him than her own situation.

He entered her room and immediately saw that at least one of his suppositions was right. She was alone.

But she was also sound asleep.

"Mimi?" he whispered.

Nothing. She didn't even stir.

He edged closer, his eyes adjusting to the low light. It was nearly dawn, and a bit of brightness was easing in through the slats in the window blinds. Enough to reveal the gleam of her red hair against the pillow and the beautiful face.

"Hey, are you really asleep?"

She mumbled something and shifted in her sleep. He leaned closer to try to hear what she was saying.

"Don't need to fly," she whispered.

"What?" He sat on the edge of the bed and reached over to smooth her hair off her brow.

Her lashes fluttered a little, but she didn't open her eyes. She was obviously dead to the world. Judging by the white streaks on her cheeks—she hadn't even washed off her makeup—she'd done some crying in the night.

His heart twisted and he called himself every name in the book. He shouldn't have left her to deal with the ambush on her own. He should have set aside his own anger and been there for her, a hand on her shoulder. Someone should have had her back.

It had been a mistake. A big one. It was also one he would never repeat, if she forgave him and let him back in her life.

He waited another moment, but she still didn't stir. Finally, figuring he ought to go back to his own place, shower, and change, he bent down and kissed her temple, then stood to leave.

"Don't go. Wait for me."

He froze. But she still didn't open her eyes, didn't move or reach for him. Was she still talking in her sleep?

"It was you. The man of my dreams."

"Mimi?" he asked, truly unsure now. Her voice sounded steady, assured.

She opened her eyes.

"Don't go," she repeated.

He smiled down at her. "I thought you were dreaming."

"I'm not, am I?" she whispered.

"No, honey, you're wide-awake."

She slowly sat up on the bed, letting the covers fall to her lap to reveal her beautiful, naked breasts, all pink and inviting. Xander's mouth went wet with want, and his other body parts went hard.

But he hadn't come here to make love to her—at least not right away. They couldn't go back to what they'd had before, couldn't keep having this amazingly sensual affair, until they at least acknowledged all the other variables in their relationship.

Emotions. Feelings. All that crap, which didn't seem so much like crap right now when his was the heart that was twisting and aching and hers were the beautiful eyes that were still luminous with many shed tears.

"I'm sorry I left," he told her. "I was wrong. I should have stayed to make sure you were all right."

"I'm fine." She moved over toward the center of the bed, pulling the covers back, beckoning him to join her.

He kicked off his shoes, but kept the rest of his clothes on, and sat down.

As if she feared he wasn't getting undressed because he was still angry, she immediately explained. "Xander, I didn't have an official conversation with Dimitri, not because I didn't want to, but because I really didn't think there was any need. We went out a couple of times, that's it. Last Saturday, when Helen showed up, I flat out told him that I didn't consider our relationship serious and that it was none of my business how he felt about her."

He had figured as much, but couldn't deny a rush of relief went through him as she confirmed it.

She wasn't finished. "I eventually realized you thought I'd actually made things even more clear than that with him, and I meant to...but he went out of town, and I didn't see him again until yesterday, when all hell broke loose."

All hell had broken loose on her yesterday. And instead of staying there, sucking up his own feelings and helping her out, he'd taken off.

It was going to take a long time to make that up to her. But he would do it, no matter what.

"Do you understand?" she asked, sounding worried.

"I absolutely understand," he told her.

"I am sorry," she insisted.

"I know."

"If it's any consolation," she added with a tiny, irrepressible grin, "he certainly got the message last night."

He chuckled. "That, I wish I had stayed to see."

"Actually, it wasn't any kind of a shock. He wasn't at all on board with that ridiculous proposal. My father had mentioned the idea to him yesterday morning, and he hadn't yet figured out how to tell him that he wasn't in love with me."

Xander suspected that was because he was still in love with someone else. Someone who lived right upstairs. But he didn't really care about Dimitri's romantic entanglements. He was only interested in his and Mimi's.

He slid his arm under her shoulders, pulling her

closer. Mimi turned onto her side, rolling against him, slipping her naked leg between his jean-clad ones. The move was both trusting and sensual. He regretted that he'd kept up his defenses by not just stripping his body as bare as hers.

But he could strip one thing bare right now—his emotions.

"I'm in love with you, Mimi," he admitted softly.

She sighed and burrowed closer. Though he couldn't see his face, he suspected there was a smile on it.

"I guess that's why I got upset last night. I have gone from closet-peeper to crazy, possessive man-in-love in just a couple of weeks, and I didn't even want to contemplate the idea that you didn't feel the same way."

She tilted her head back to look up at him. Lifting her hand, she brushed her fingers across his mouth, as if forbidding him to say such a thing. He kissed them gently, softly, curling his cheek into her palm.

"I love you, too," she told him. "I hadn't wanted to say anything for the same reasons—it was too fast, went against all common sense. But I am completely in love with you, Xander. You've become the most important thing in my life, and I'll move heaven and earth to make sure we have a chance at happiness."

So relieved he could hardly think, he settled for bending down to kiss her. Mimi's mouth opened to him, sweet and warm, and their tongues met in a slow, hungry exploration. She wrapped her arms around his neck, and he stroked her bare back, holding her close.

He would eventually strip out of his clothes and make love to her, but for right now, holding her, kissing her, whispering words he hadn't ever dreamed he'd say, much less hear, was enough.

Still, he was curious about one thing. And after another long kiss, that curiosity made him ask, "What were you dreaming about right before you woke up?"

A slow smile spread across her face. "I remember this time…I haven't remembered my last few dreams, but this one is so clear." She pressed a kiss against his chest, nibbling her way up to his neck. "I dreamed I was stuck in a boring, stifling old castle, and the king was trying to drag me down to marry someone, only I didn't want to get married."

He laughed softly. "Talk about dreams reflecting life!"

"Exactly. Then a mysterious man wrapped in shadows appeared. He told me I didn't have to stay, said I could step right out my window to the world that was waiting for me."

"And did you? Did you go with him?"

"I woke up right before the dream ended."

She moved closer to kiss him again. But right before their lips met, she added, "But to answer your question…yes, I did. I went with him. And the world was beautiful."

Epilogue

IF ANNA'S TALENT with backyard engagement parties was amazing, her ability to put together a small, private wedding was absolutely without equal. As Mimi stood beside the man she loved, promising to share with him all the days of her life, she realized she couldn't have ever dreamed of a more perfect place to exchange the vows that would tie her to Xander forever.

They stood at the edge of the woods under a gazebo draped with soft white netting. Starlight and dozens of candles provided all the illumination they needed. They were serenaded by the whisper of the autumn breeze through the ancient trees, whose leaves were just now turning gold, orange and red.

Though they had wanted this event small, private and genuine, they were still surrounded by well-wishers. Their friends and neighbors—Anna and Obi-Wan, of course. Will, the writer, who'd sworn he was going to have to write a book about all the romantic shenanigans that went on in the great old house. Helen and Tuck…and with them, Dimitri, who held tightly on to the hands of both his future wife and his future stepson.

And Mimi's parents.

Her father hadn't walked her down the aisle...but he *had* walked her across the lawn. The grass had been her aisle, the backdrop of trees was their cathedral.

It had taken a few months for him to come around to everything. Mimi going to work for a department store chain had been hard enough, though she'd stuck to her guns despite almost constant harassment and pleading.

Her marrying not a future king of Wall Street, but a heroic prince who risked his life on a daily basis to help others, had been an even higher hill to climb. But it appeared even stubborn, spoiled, bossy millionaires were able to be swayed by genuine emotion, and to recognize what they had before they lost it forever.

He never said it, but she strongly suspected that what Xander had said to her father that night when he'd given her that ultimatum had finally sunk through his thick skull. Because the look he had given her as he passed her hand over to Xander's, in front of the minister marrying them in the eyes of God and nature, had been misty, emotional and filled with love.

It had been the final wish she'd made before the wedding, knowing his acceptance and approval—which she'd already gotten from her mother, who'd loved Xander at first sight—would mean the world to her.

"Mimi and Xander, congratulations, I now pronounce you husband and wife."

As the minister spoke the final words of the service, the breeze suddenly picked up, blowing her hair wildly around her face. Nearly all the candles were winked out, and the evening descended into darkness. But then, as if the love that welled up between her and Xander had electrified the night, every firefly in the woods chose that moment to brighten the world.

"I knew it," she whispered, smiling. "I knew love made them glow."

"In that case, Hermione Burdette McKinley," Xander said as he bent toward her for a kiss to seal their union, "we're never going to be in darkness again."

* * * * *

Want to know what happened
to Lauren at her high school reunion?
Look for next month's Blaze release,
THE GUY MOST LIKELY TO...!

PASSION

COMING NEXT MONTH

AVAILABLE JUNE 26, 2012

#693 LEAD ME HOME

Sons of Chance

Vicki Lewis Thompson

Matthew Tredway has made a name for himself as a world-class horse trainer. Only, after one night with Aurelia Smith, he's the one being led around by the nose....

#694 THE GUY MOST LIKELY TO...

A Blazing Hot Summer Read

Leslie Kelly, Janelle Denison and Julie Leto

Every school has one. That special guy, the one every girl had to have or they'd just die! Did you ever wonder what happened to him? Come back to school with three of Blaze's bestselling authors and find out how great the nights are after the glory days are over....

#695 TALL, DARK & RECKLESS

Heather MacAllister

After interviewing a thousand men, dating coach Piper Scott knows handsome daredevil foreign journalist Mark Banning is definitely not her type—but what if he's her perfect man?

#696 NO HOLDS BARRED

Forbidden Fantasies

Cara Summers

Defense attorney Piper MacPherson is being threatened by a stalker and protected by FBI profiler Duncan Sutherland. Her problem? She's not sure which is more dangerous....

#697 BREATHLESS ON THE BEACH

Flirting with Justice

Wendy Etherington

When PR exec Victoria Holmes attends a client's beach-house party, she has no idea there'll be cowboys—well, one cowboy. Lucky for Victoria, Jarred McKenna's not afraid to get a little wet....

#698 NO GOING BACK

Uniformly Hot!

Karen Foley

Army Special Ops commando Chase Rawlins has been trained to handle anything. Only, little does he guess how much he'll enjoy "handling" sexy publicist Kate Fitzgerald!

New York Times *and* USA TODAY *bestselling author Vicki Lewis Thompson returns with yet another irresistible cowpoke! Meet Mathew Tredway—cowboy, horse whisperer and honorary Son of Chance.*

Read on for a sneak peek from the bestselling miniseries SONS OF CHANCE:

LEAD ME HOME
Available July 2012 only from Harlequin® Blaze™.

AS MATTHEW RETURNED to the corral and Houdini, the taste of Aurelia's mouth was on his lips and her scent clung to his clothes. He'd briefly satisfied the craving growing within him, and like a light snack before a meal, it would have to do.

When he'd first walked into the kitchen, his mind had been occupied with the challenge of training Houdini. He'd thought his concentration would hold long enough to get some carrots, ask about the corn bread and leave before succumbing to Aurelia's appeal. He'd miscalculated. Within a very short time, desire had claimed every brain cell.

Although seducing her this morning was out of the question, his libido had demanded some sort of satisfaction. He'd tried to deny that urge and had nearly made it out of the house. Apparently his willpower was no match for the temptation of Aurelia's mouth, though, and he'd turned around.

If he'd ever felt this kind of desperate need for a woman, he couldn't recall it. During the night, as he'd lain in his narrow bunk listening to the cowhands snore, he'd searched for an explanation as to why Aurelia affected him this way.

Sometime in the early-morning hours he'd come up with

the answer. After years of dating women who were rolling stones like he was, he'd developed an itch for a hearth-and-home kind of woman. Aurelia, with her cooking skills and voluptuous body, could give him that.

With luck, once he'd scratched this particular itch, he'd be fine again. He certainly hoped so, because he had no intention of giving up his career, and travel was a built-in requirement. Plus he liked to travel and had no real desire to stay in one spot and become domesticated.

Tonight he'd say all that to Aurelia, because he didn't want her going into this with any illusions about permanence. He figured that when the right guy came along, she'd get married and have kids.

Too bad that guy wouldn't be him....

Will Aurelia be the one to corral this cowboy for good?
Find out in: LEAD ME HOME

Available July 2012
wherever Harlequin® Blaze™ books are sold.

HBEXP0712